Spring Break Adventure

Jessica Yellowknife

Illustrations by Marvin Alonso

Order this book online at www.trafford.com
or email orders@trafford.com

Most Trafford titles are also available at major online book retailers.

Illustrations by Marvin Alonso.

Printed in the United States of America.

ISBN: 978-1-4269-6952-2 (sc)

Trafford rev. 06/28/2011

 www.trafford.com

North America & international
toll-free: 1 888 232 4444 (USA & Canada)
phone: 250 383 6864 ♦ fax: 812 355 4082

Contents

In memory of my grandpa

Joe Jacques 2010

Chapter One

A MAGICAL SPRING BREAK

It was the first day of spring break, and two kids were just getting up to start the day.

"Oh, look, I think it's going to be a gorgeous day. I can even smell the fresh fragrance of flowers blossoming," Alyssa said out loud. She looked out the window, admiring the view and feeling the magic of spring break. Having no school for a whole week wasn't bad either. *Is it reality or just a dream?* She wondered.

Alyssa put on her slippers and quietly slithered down the hall to her little brother Jack's room. She was hoping to terrify him by giving him an early morning scare. The two little devils were always pulling tricks on each other to see who would be the first one to crawl to Mom like a big baby. Alyssa thought she would be sweet for once and gave her little brother a wet Willy, which usually made him jump up and wonder what was wrong with his sister.

They raced down the front stairs past the living room through the dining room, and into the kitchen. They were both breathing hard when they found their mother, Susan, making their breakfast. Susan was just about ready to call them for their breakfast. As she picked up a plate, she told them that their breakfast was on the countertop. "Don't forget to take a glass of orange juice," she insisted. Their plates were quickly full of yummy pancakes with lots of crispy bacon.

While Susan drank her favourite morning coffee, she glanced over at the children. *Such beautiful kids*, she thought to herself, *yet they seem so different from each other.* It wasn't just in their appearances but more in their attitude toward life. When she looked at Jack, she saw a clean-cut, brown-haired boy, slight of build but full of energy, curiosity, living with reality of himself.

Alyssa, she noticed, was growing so fast. Her hair was straight and dark brown, and soon, she would have her shape if she kept her from sleeping all the time. *Her little dreamer,* she thought to herself.

"So what is on the agenda for you guys today?"

Jack and Alyssa looked at each other. It had slipped their minds. They had forgotten to plan anything fun to do while they were on their spring break. After a little bit of table arguing between the two kids, who were soon stopped by their mother, Jack decided on playing with his toy train collection. Alyssa, however, couldn't decide on what to do. Alyssa gazed at her mother, who was busy cleaning up the breakfast dishes. She wanted to ask her mom for some advice on what she could do.

Susan was scrambling about. She seemed to be doing a million things at once. There was so much to do, cleaning, getting ready for work, and planning in her mind for a big office party later that day. She paused and explained to Alyssa, "I'm really busy at the moment, honey. Can we talk about this later, dear?"

Alyssa decided to go to her bedroom. She turned on some music and stretched out on her bed. She let her mind wander, not really able to come to a conclusion about what she wanted to accomplish on her first day of spring break. Even with all the dolls and toys piled up in her room, she could not think of anything interesting to do.

Meanwhile, Jack was happily playing with his trains. He wanted to keep busy so that he didn't bother his mother while she worked. Jack was putting the finishing touches on his train track when his sister, Alyssa, entered the room. Jack was so busy concentrating that he didn't even notice her. He continued on with his work. Alyssa watched from the living room doorway. She couldn't help but notice her brother was enjoying himself and not paying much attention to what was going on around him. At first, she thought, *what fun it would be if Jack and I could play together*. Then she remembered how they truly got along only a few moments ago at the breakfast table. Like vinegar and olive oil, they didn't mix well. Trouble always happened when the two decided to play together.

Alyssa hesitated, looking directly at Jack, who was playfully enjoying himself. She decided to head back toward her bedroom. She stretched out on her bed once again. Thoughts soon came to her mind as she remembered about her favourite hockey team, the Ottawa Gladiators.

She curled up, comfortable on her bed, enjoying the warmth of the bed sheets. Her eyelids became heavy, and soon, she closed her eyes and fell into a deep sleep. Her long brown hair mingled with the pillow. Thoughts flew through her mind. The little dreamer decided then and there that she had a magnificent idea! She would go watch her favourite hockey team play in Ottawa. But how would she get there, and what would she take with her? As she tossed slightly on her bed and snuggled up to her pillow, she made a mental list of things that she would need.

She would surely need a backpack to put everything in. Soon, she was in the process of organizing everything for the big trip. Now she was ready for her big journey to see her favourite team in Ottawa ... or was she?

Alyssa continued to stretch out on her bed, thinking deep thoughts about what she might have forgotten. *As soon as I get my bicycle, I'm on my way,* she thought. Imagination set in as she felt the comfort of the bed.

Now dreaming, Alyssa jumped onto her bike, and away she went. Now she was ready to start her voyage to see the Gladiators play hockey. Alyssa turned the handlebars and steered her bike northward toward Ottawa. Soon, she left her hometown of Kingston far behind. As she followed close alongside the bike path, she admired the view. While she traveled down the path, she saw a flock of geese cresting over the horizon out of the corner of her eye. Excitement filled her up as Alyssa journeyed along the narrow path to Ottawa.

She rode past some children who were having a kite competition to see who could fly their kites the highest in the light blue, cloudless sky towering high above them. Alyssa glanced at all the beautiful kites as they soared above, each of them with multi-colored patterns decorating the blue sky.

Nearby, she could see some boys fishing. She stop her bike, watching curiously as they baited their hooks and cast their fishing lines out into the bubbling brook close to a nearby embankment. The water ran swiftly beside the bike path. A gasp of surprise came out of her mouth as she watched one of the boys catch a small pike. It took some mighty pulling with his fishing rod, but he eventually pulled the flopping fish out of the bubbling brook and placed it onto the soft green grass. *Cool,* she thought. She watched the boys as they did a mighty victory dance, circling alongside the small brook.

Alyssa glanced around to see what else was happening. She noticed a family of ducks swimming nearby, the birds happily chirping away in a nest high up in a large elm tree. As she continued to glance around her, she noticed a woman who was tall with long blonde hair. She was wearing a pink jogging suit. The woman was bent down, for she seemed to be exhausted.

Alyssa slowed down, parked her bike, and walked over to the young woman, smiling to greet her.

"Hi there, my name is Alyssa. What's your name?"

"Howdy, my name is Jo-Anne. Alyssa, it's very nice to make your acquaintance!"

"Do you need anything, Jo-Anne?"

"No thanks! Well, on second thought. I am a little thirsty."

"I have some water in my bottle. You can help yourself to it, Jo-Anne, if you would like," she said as she handed over her water bottle.

"Thanks!"

They chatted for a while. Alyssa discovered that Jo-Anne was training hard for the Olympics. That was awesome. *It's not every day you get to meet an Olympic athlete,* Alyssa thought. Then she said farewell to Jo-Anne and wished her all the best and was soon on her way.

Susan was in the kitchen preparing lunch for the kids. She was fixing up some mushroom soup with ham and cheese sandwiches. "Kids, it's lunchtime," Susan shouted as she put the sandwiches on the countertop.

Alyssa could hear her mother calling, but she quietly rolled over on her bed, drifting back into her daydream. Jack walked over and tapped softly on his sister's bedroom door. He slowly opened the door and prepared to duck in case she tossed something at him. He crept over to the bed and then screeched in his sister's ear.

"Didn't you hear mom? It's lunchtime."

He received no response from Alyssa. Jack shook his head and then went downstairs and headed toward the living room to start cleaning up his mess. He sat down on the tall stool, propped his elbows on the countertop in the kitchen, and hungrily ate his lunch. After he left the dishes on the countertop, he walked over to his mother at the dining room table and snuggled his head into her shoulder.

"Sissy is in outer space," Jack joked to his mother.

"She'll come out when she's famished. What are you going to do this afternoon, Jack?"

"Well, I was thinking of going to the library to do some investigation on the solar system for a project that I'm working on. Afterward, I'm heading over to the park to play with some of my friends."

"Oh, okay, be careful though."

After lunch, Jack grabbed an umbrella and raced out the door. He walked about three blocks from his house and met up with his best friend, Paige. Jack asked Paige if she would join him at the library to do some research on a secret project. He hoped to fabricate a train that could run off the solar energy of the sun so that it would protect the environment from pollution.

Paige agreed to help out on the secret project. They had always been best friends, and like best buddies. They strolled down the sidewalk toward the library.

When they opened the huge doors at the large, brown, brick library, Jack and Paige headed straight toward the index card stand. Paige began to look through the reference cards about trains while Jack started looking up everything he could about solar energy. *Lots*, he thought to himself, *solar panels and solar plexus, solar sail, the solar system, and solar wind.* Jack decided not to research the solar plexus, because it was about the network of nerve tissue and fibres at the lower part of the stomach. Jack began his research with the following:

Solar Energy:
Solar energy is the energy that can be produced from the sun's rays or the effects of the sun's rays.

Solar Panel:
A solar panel is a bank of light-sensitive solar cells used to generate electricity.

Solar Sail:
A solar sail is a flat sail attached to a moveable object, and it is used to receive propulsive force from the sun's radiation.

Solar System:
The solar system is the sun and all of the heavenly bodies revolving around it.

Solar Winds:
Solar winds are the charged particles emitted from the sun's surface.

After they researched for a while, Jack decided that he only wanted to explore information about solar panels and the solar sails for now. Jack then found Paige, who was busy researching trains and how they operated. Jack took her notes and photocopied them. He then added Paige's notes to his notes for later research.

Paige and Jack start out to the "Hop and Go," a marvellous store located down the block that had everything a kid could ask for. Together, they found that they had enough loose change to share a strawberry milk shake. As they used two straws, they sipped away at the drink and hung out for a while, enjoying each other's company. Later, they both suggested that they head out toward the nearby park, where they each loved to play.

Still deep in her daydream, Alyssa hopped on her bike and proceeded down the path. Up and down the hills she went, crossing over several bridges and admiring the view as she steered her bike along the pavement of the bike path.

This is fun. Up and down and over the hills, I go. Wee, Alyssa thought. All of the sudden, she stopped. She heard something in the distance. *What could it be?* she wondered. She moved closer to the sound, and she soon found that it was actually a whimpering sound. Someone was crying, but who was out there?

"Is anybody out there?" she cried out.

Alyssa got off her bike and began to explore the area around her. As she listened, she could hear a muffled, soft whimper. She was really determined to find out who was whimpering. Walking softly, she came across a pile of twigs, and there, sticking out of the pile of twigs, was a pair of tiny red sneakers. She tossed the twigs aside as fast as she could and hurried to rescue whoever was stuck.

To her surprise, it was a scared little boy who seemed to be around four years old. Alyssa stood back and looked over the young child. She could see that he was dreadfully banged up. Carefully, she stretched out her hand to the little boy.

"Hi there, my name is Alyssa. I'm a friend. What is your name?"

The frighten boy was unsure of what to do. He was very reluctant to answer. He had always been told not to talk to strangers. He was alone and lost, and he didn't know what to do. He decided to take a chance and trust Alyssa.

"My name is Matthew, and I'm lost. But it's nice to meet you, Alyssa."

"Where are your mom and dad?"

"I don't know. I can't find them. I was playing with my sisters, and I got lost. It seemed like they vanished into thin air."

"Oh, I see. We should try to find them, don't you agree? But first we should mend those cuts and bruises."

Alyssa fetched her first-aid kit out of her knapsack and started to mend Matthew's injuries. She grabbed a warm wool sweater and placed it on Matthew to keep him warm. As she looked into her magic knapsack, she found some freshly wrapped macaroni-and-cheese sandwiches and offered one to Matthew. She could see that he was very hungry. She watched him as he gobbled up the sandwich.

After lunch, they quickly cleaned up their mess. To relax him, they both played a game of hide-and-seek. This appeared to be Matthew's favourite game to play. After some time had passed, Alyssa stopped and told Matthew that they should get started on looking for his family, because they would be worried sick about him. "It will be dark soon, too," she said, "so we should get started."

Alyssa grabbed her knapsack, pulled up her bike, and pushed off the kickstand. She placed Matthew on the handlebars and began to ride off. She asked Matthew how he had gotten to where they were. He said he had been running away from a racoon and had fallen into the trap of twigs. Alyssa could see two bike paths as she rode toward them.

"Matthew, which way?"

"I can't remember."

"Try to remember. Matthew you can it."

Matthew closed his eyes really tight. He searched and searched his mind, trying to remember something. Then he remembered a tree with a huge red X on it.

"That's excellent. Do you see anything else?"

"I'm thinking. I'm thinking. There is a pair of red-and-white sneakers high up in a pine tree way down the path."

Alyssa looked closely at the two pathways. After she examined each pathway for some time, she decided that they looked the same and proceeded left. Some of the trees along the way were slowly dying, their leaves littering the ground. They had seen better days—that was for sure. The two friends headed down the pathway. Alyssa was unsure of where she was going and hoped that Matthew could show her the way. She wanted to make sure he arrived home safe and sound. She imagined that he was scared, not knowing where his parents were, and that his parents had to be worried sick with fright, not knowing where Matthew was.

All of the sudden, Matthew started jumping up and down on the handlebars. Matthew started screaming at the top of his lungs. "We're going the right way! We're going the right way, Alyssa!"

"That's great. Let's keep an eye open for those sneakers now."

Approximately, a mile down the bike path, Alyssa could see the red-and-white sneakers hanging from a pine tree. Alyssa pulled her bike to a halt.

"Now where do we go?"

"I don't know. I can't remember!"

"Well, let's take a tiny break and have a nice snack while we try to figure out which direction we should proceed with next."

As the two friends sat down and began to enjoy their snack and sipped on some orange juice, Alyssa could hear someone whimpering again. *Now who could that be?* She wondered to herself. After she peeked both ways, she began to search around them. Matthew just looked at Alyssa with a funny face and wondered what she was doing.

"Can't you hear that? Doesn't it sound like someone is crying?"

Alyssa began searching again. Matthew turned his head in the opposite direction.

"Daddy, Daddy, we found you."

" Who are we?" Matthew's dad questioned.

Oh! You mean my new best friend Alyssa. She helped me find you. She mended my cuts and bruises and shared some of her food with me. She even put this sweater on me. After that, we played hide-and-seek. Now she helped me find you."

"She sounds like a good friend to me. Where is she now?"

"I don't know. Alyssa, Alyssa, over here, it's my daddy."

As Alyssa walked over to Matthew and his father, it started to rain. "Hi there, thanks for everything."

"You're welcome. It was my pleasure. Matthew's a great kid. He's a very pleasant and well-mannered little boy. You must be very proud of him."

"Your mother and your sisters are worried sick about you, Matthew. Alyssa, how would you like to come too? You could get out of this rain."

"I really would appreciate that," she said. "Thanks."

"It's not far from here, so let's get started. It's not much, but its home to us."

Alyssa couldn't believe her eyes. They were living in an old train tunnel for shelter. They had no electricity, heat, or food to eat. They only had each other and nothing else. She found this hard to believe. She had never realized that people actuality lived like this. Alyssa didn't know what to say or do first. She didn't want to offend anyone by what she might say or do.

"Well, first thing's first! Let's get a nice, big, roaring fire going. It will keep us warm and dry from the storm." She suggested.

Alyssa began to demonstrate how to start a fire by rubbing two sticks together until there was a spark and a little smoke, and a warm fire was soon on its way. Afterward, she put up her tiny tent in the corner of the tunnel.

She took her sleeping bag and wrapped it around the two tiny girls, who were shivering together in the farthest corner of the tunnel. She went back to her magical knapsack and took out some food and passed it out to the family, which was watching her very closely. After dinner, the children climbed into her tent and snuggled together in the sleeping bag and fell fast asleep.

"How can we ever repay you for all that you have done for us?" asked Matthew's father.

"There is no payment needed. All I want is your friendship."

"Thank you just the same. If you ever need anything, just ask. Okay!" said Matt's mom very sincerely.

"Okay, it's a deal!"

Alyssa told Matthew's parents that she was on her way to Ottawa to watch her favourite hockey team, the Ottawa Gladiators, play some hockey.

Meanwhile, Jack and Paige arrived at Harvey Park. They splashed in the mud puddles and climbed to the top of the jungle gym. They jumped off, flapping their arms, hoping that the solar power would make them fly like the birds in the sky. In reality, however, it didn't work. They decided to try some tinfoil on their arms and try again. Once again, it was a flop. It was starting to get late. Jack told Paige that they would work on their invention from their homes. They could compare notes in the morning, and soon, they were on their way home for their suppers.

When Jack arrived home, he quietly opened the front door and walked into the house. He put his notes and library books on a nearby chair with his wet umbrella. He noticed that his mom had done the lunch dishes. Jack started to search for his mom to let her know that he was back from the park. Then he remembered that she had an office party that she was going to and would be heading out soon. *Mom probably had a hot bubble bath going,* he thought. *I wonder what dress she'll be wearing this evening. I hope it's her black-and-red dress. She looks fantastic in it.*

"I'm home from the park, Mom," he shouted as he went from room to room until he found her. She was in the den, typing quickly on the computer.

Jack saw that she had already put on her makeup and curled her beautiful, long, black hair and put it up in a banana comb. She had put on his favourite dress for the occasion. Jack had always loved his mother's long hair, which hung past her hips. Sometimes she allowed him to brush her hair, because she knew that Jack loved brushing it.

Energetically, Jack said, "Hi, mom, I'm back from the park."

"Jack go clean-up for dinner!"

The doorbell then rang. Susan answered the door. It was Zoë, the babysitter.

"I know I'm ahead of schedule. I hope you don't mind," Zoë said to Susan.

"Come on in. I'm still getting ready. Zoë, can you finish getting dinner ready?"

"No problem. Is it in the oven?"

"Yeah, it is. Thanks."

"That's why I came early, to be of some assistance to you in case you need it." She was always helpful.

"Jack is in the washroom, cleaning up. Alyssa is in her room. She's been there all day fantasizing about something. I'd just leave her alone. She'll come out when she's hungry. Could you put a plate of food in the microwave for her and leave a note on the dining room table telling her where her supper is. Oh, one more thing. Can you ask her to take a bath before she goes to bed tonight? Thanks."

"Hi, Zoë, how would you like to help me with my invention after supper?" said Jack enthusiastically.

"Sure, sound entertaining. What are we inventing?"

"It's top secret—shhh!"

"See you guys later this evening. Farewell," said Susan on her way out the door.

Zoë and Jack soon sat down to enjoy their dinner. Afterward, Jack helped with the dinner dishes. He then walked up the stairs to his bedroom and started to search for some sketches and some sketching paper that he had. He headed back to the living room, where he found his notes and books from the library. He carefully laid out everything in front of himself and called Zoë for her help.

Alyssa finally came out of her bedroom and proceeded into the living room to see what everybody else was doing.

"Hi, Alyssa, your dinner is in the microwave. Then your mom wants you to take a bath after your dinner."

Alyssa walked over to the kitchen and grabbed her dinner from the microwave. After she was finished eating, she proceeded to have a nice, steaming hot bubble bath with a hint of lavender.

Alyssa went back to the living room to help in cleaning up the materials for Jack's invention. Afterward, they all enjoyed playing a game called Sorry. Of course, Jack won like usual.

Zoë advanced into the kitchen and come back with some candles and marshmallows. Zoë turned out the lights and lit the candles. She handed out forks and marshmallows to the children to roast over the candles.

Zoë sat down to join the children as they roasted their marshmallows. She then began to tell them a ghost story called "The Babysitter."

"The babysitter's name was Mary-Ann, and she heard a sound coming from upstairs, where the children were fast asleep. Mary-Ann went upstairs. The sound grew louder and louder as she got closer to the children's room. Scrape, scrape, scrape was all she heard. She stopped at the children's bedroom door. She reached for the doorknob. Her hand trembled. Her heart pounded, and sweat poured from her face. She slowly turned the doorknob and opened the door—"

Then Zoë gasped for effect before she continued, "The children were safely in their beds. Mary-Ann looked a little more closely. They didn't have any faces! Just a pool of mushy goo! Mary-Ann screamed loudly. She turned around ready to run, but there was a big hair guy ... standing right in front of her. He raised his right arm. There was a big metal hook where his hand should have been. The man took his hook and went after the babysitter!"

Zoë then made another scraping noise.

"That was the end of the children and the babysitters ... boo!"

"Did I scare you?" Zoë then asked.

"No!" They replied, but they were both trembling slightly.

"Well, It's time for you two to go to bed. I'll see you both when you wake up in the morning."

"Okay. Good night, Zoë."

Off to bed they went. Jack fell right into forty winks, but Alyssa had trouble dozing off. Thoughts kept scampering about in her brain. *I can't sleep,* she thought. *I keep trying, but ... nothing is working. Maybe some lukewarm milk might do the trick.*

"Zoë, May I come down and grab some milk?"

"Certainly, why can't you sleep, Alyssa?"

"No, everything is racing though my brain."

"Oh, Why is that?"

"I just can't put anything into place."

"I see. Want to talk about it with me? It might help."

"Where should I start?"

"Oh, I don't know. What was your last thought? That would be a great place to start, don't you think?"

"Oh, that's easy. It was Mom. I'm always thinking about her. I am also concerned about her a great deal, too."

"Why is that? Your mom seems to be cheerful enough."

"Not really. It may look like she is, but she puts up a wonderful front. Sometimes I hear her crying at night, and sometimes I see her wishing upon a star. The only real time I really see Mom happy is when she is doing something amusing with my brother or me. When the three of us are doing exciting things together, that is when she is truly happy. When she has a conversation with someone about a certain man or when he's around, she lights up like a Christmas tree. No other man has ever had this kind of response from her. I call him 'the waver.' Ever since I was a baby, he's been there waving to us. If mom is in trouble, he's right there. He doesn't say a word to her, but he lets her know that he's always nearby. It's magical to witness the twinkle that comes into her eyes. It's similar to a little star that lights up the midnight sky. That has to be some kind of special love, right?"

"When two people fall in love, they describe it exactly the way you are describing it about your mom and this man. How did they meet?"

"She became acquainted with him sixteen years ago. Whatever happened on that day is a mystery to me. I'll never really know. All moms will tell us if a man does exactly what he did on that very day. That one special thing that spread him from all the other guys she would marry him in a heartbeat. She hopes that they will meet each other again someday. Whatever happened in that room on that very day seems to have had a lasting effect on her that will last a lifetime? I remember she walked out of that room, looked at my godfather, and said that she would marry that man someday."

"How would Susan describe the man you call 'the waver,' Alyssa?"

"Mom says he's a true gentleman. She fell hard for him on the first time they met each other. No other man has ever come close to him, even today that is. She always said Jack and I make her happy, but this is different. It's like watching two school-age kids with puppy love in the eyes. It's priceless to watch. When the two of them are in the same room—it doesn't matter where it is—you can see what I'm saying. Neither one has ever gotten married, even to this day. He still can get Mom to turn her thought. It doesn't even matter who is around. Mom tells me it's because a gentleman calls on the lady, and with this guy, he's very bashful. You have to see them together to know this. Mom is very patient. She does her own thing. Maybe someday the two of them will eventually make contact with each other once again." Stated Alyssa

"Who knows what will happen?" Zoe replied.

"You could ask more about this guy with Mom if you wish. Then you can see for yourself how her face lights up when she speaks about him. All I know is no other man has ever come close to her heart. Well, beside Jack that is. She never wanted our father, just us. Mom said she had her whole life planned out when she was seven years old. So far, she has accomplished everything, except getting married to her soul mate. She's not in a hurry, either. Mom said that someday she'll get married or say she's still looking for the right one. Do you agree, Zoë?"

"Sure, sounds great to me. Is there anything else that is bothering you? You should try to get some sleep before your mother gets home."

"Okay, I will give it another try. Thank for listening, Zoë."

Alyssa finished her milk and then put her glass in the dishwasher. She headed back upstairs to her bedroom. She lay down on her bed once again. Slowly, she started to drift back into her fantasy world once again.

Zoë tidied up around the house and then walked into the den and began to make up her bed on the sofa for the night. Suddenly, she became aware of the children's mother, Susan, coming up the walkway to the front entrance.

"Did you have a good time, Susan?"

"I certainly did. But it's late, and I have to go to bed now. I have a busy day tomorrow. Were the children good for you?"

"Yeah, there was no problem tonight."

"You're welcome to spend the night if you wish. Well, good night. See you in the morning."

Chapter Two

DWARFS AND MUD PUDDLES

It was six in the morning, and the sunrise was coming up over the horizon. As Susan was getting up, she stumbles over a pile of clothes that she had left on the floor. When she headed for her morning shower, she found the water was steaming hot. It felt so relaxing all over her aching muscles. After she tossed on her bathrobe, she staggered downstairs for her morning coffee. *Thank goodness for coffee timers*, she thought to herself. After she poured herself a cup of coffee, she began to sip on it. Susan was sitting at the dining room table in a daze, as if something or someone had impressed her during the night.

Alyssa was standing in the doorway of the dining room, watching her mother staring into space. This wasn't like her mother. So she started to speculate about what was on her mother's mind this morning. What might have happened at the party the night before?

"Did you enjoy yourself last night?" There was no response from her mother. Alyssa softly tapped on her mother's shoulder.

"Did you enjoy yourself last night?" she inquired again.

"Oh! What did you say, sweetie?"

"Did you enjoy yourself last night?" she repeated once again.

"Yes, I did. I had a wonderful time. Thanks for asking. How would you like it if I made you a Spanish omelette for breakfast, sweetie?"

"That sounds great, Mom."

Susan got up and went over to the refrigerator. She took out some eggs, milk, cheese slices, ham, green peppers, and onions. She chopped up the green pepper, ham, and the onions into tiny pieces. She mixed the ingredients along with the eggs and milk in a bowl. She whipped it all together and then poured it into another bowl. Last but not least, she added some cheese slices on top. Gently, she positioned the bowl into the microwave oven.

"Oh my," Susan said as she glanced at the time. "I'm going to be late for work." She continued getting dressed for work as she reached for her briefcase. She told Alyssa to be good, and out the door she raced.

"That was weird!" Alyssa said out loud as she took her omelette from the microwave. She sat down at the dining room table and started to eat her breakfast. Jack grabbed some frosted flake cereal, milk, and orange juice and then sat down next to Alyssa.

"Good morning, Alyssa! What is weird?" he said in a sarcastic tone.

"Oh! Nothing! Eat your breakfast," she mumbled back. "What's on your agenda for today?" Alyssa probed.

"Not sure. Why? What's on your agenda?" he quizzed.

"Oh, I'm not sure yet. I might just go back to bed again, or at least that's what I'm thinking of doing anyway."

"What are you thinking about anyway?"

"None of your business," she snarled back.

Jack just stared at Alyssa for a moment as Zoë walked into the dining room. Jack shrugged one of his shoulders, not quite understanding his sister.

"Well, I'll leave you ladies now. I'm off to the library to work on my invention," Jack said as he quickly opened the front door and raced outside into the fresh air. Alyssa stared at the mess on the kitchen table and started cleaning up the breakfast dishes.

"Zoë, if there is anything that you need, don't hesitate to knock on my bedroom door. Well, I'm off to my bedroom now."

"Okay, Alyssa."

Alyssa jump up off the dining room chair without any hesitation taking the stairs two at a time to her room. She stood in front of her bedroom window and took a quick glimpse out at the view that she had seen so many time. Slowly, she took a deep breath and let out a little sigh of relief.

"Now where was I? Oh! Yeah, I remember now," she said out loud as she climbed into her comfortable bed and slowly drifted off to sleep.

Alyssa said farewell to Matthew and his family and headed north of the train tunnel.

She continued through the woods along the path. "Oh, dear, I have a flat tire! Now what else can go wrong today?" she said. She gathered up her things, leaving her bike behind, and started walking. *This'll probably take forever*, Alyssa thought as she skipped down the path, singing to herself. She was deep in the forest when she came across four tiny bungalows, which looked like forts for children. She then noticed one of the bungalows had some smoke coming out of one tiny chimney.

Alyssa walked over to the tiny bungalow just as it started to rain, and then she knocked on the small door. The bungalow was as tall as she was. She was expecting to find children playing there. Instead, she found a family of little people. Alyssa had never met a dwarf before. She had heard about them, but she had never stumbled upon any in her lifetime.

There was a set of quintets. The little girls were all identical. Each stood two feet high and weighed about thirty-five pounds. They wore black ringlets in their hair, and they had the most beautiful hazel eyes. All of them had on pink-and-white polka-dotted dress, each with black dress shoes, too.

The five tiny girls ran around Alyssa in a circle. They stopped for a moment and stared at the giant in front of them, their mouth hanging wide open. With the girls, there was also a set of twin boys. They were a bit larger than the girls, standing at three feet tall and weighing about forty-five pounds each. They were clean-cut, and they had midnight black hair; however, their eyes were brown instead of hazel. Each of them wore a pair of coveralls with a blue shirt, and they had black dress shoes on their feet.

"Who are you?" they all inquired at the same time.

"Hi, I'm Alyssa. I don't mean to be rude, but how come you all look alike and so tiny? I've never met anyone your size before." Alyssa inquired, looking at the dwarfs.

All the dwarfs start to giggle. "How come you are so tall?" they asked. "Isn't it the same thing? Would you like to come inside our house, Alyssa? You can get out of the rain before you get soak."

Alyssa looked at the dwarf whose name was Jason and told him that she would give it a try. Alyssa entered the tiny bungalow, squeezing her way through the small doorway. Inside, she looked like she was all curled up into a ball. The dwarfs all laughed, grabbing their bellies and rolling around as they watched Alyssa trying to get comfortable in the tiny bungalow.

"This won't work," Alyssa finally said.

Everybody then climbed out of the bungalow. "Now what are we to do?" Nicole, a cute little dwarf, asked as she climbed out and started to think out loud. "I've got it. Let's establish a wall over there between those two pine trees, and we could add a small roof onto it," she eventually replied.

Alyssa had never seen anyone move so quickly in all her life—big or small, that is.

People would surely be amazed by how quickly dwarfs could move. After they had Alyssa's place ready, they started a roaring fire. The eight of them then sat around the blazing fire. Mary and Amy, two cute dwarfs, headed into one of the bungalows and brought back some refreshments. The two had brought back all kind of neat things that they could roast over the open fire and plenty of things to drink. They had corn on a cob, marshmallows, hot dogs, and fresh berry juice.

Mary and Amy handed out the food to everyone as they each took turns telling ghost stories, jokes, and sometimes just talking about nothing at all. Everyone was laughing so hard that their ribs hurt, and some of them fell over backward.

After a couple of hours flew by, Alyssa decided it was time for her to continue on with her journey. She bent over and thanked her new friends for being so generous and gave them each a hug, saying farewell to all of them. She then grabbed her backpack and continued on her journey once again.

Jack went to the library to do some more research on his invention. He just couldn't concentrate on what he was doing. He decided to take a visit to his best friend Mark's place. *Maybe we could go out and find some trouble like usual*, he thought. When he arrived at Mark's, Paige was also there to his surprise. *Even better*, Jack thought to himself, *both of my best friends are here together.*

The three friends decided to play a game of marbles, but this didn't last very long. The three friends talked about what they each would like to do. They decided on going down to the train tracks and take a look around. They all headed out of Mark's house and jumped onto their ten-speed bikes. Soon, they were headed toward the train tracks nearby.

They stopped at an old train station and parked their bikes. They gave the impression that they were searching for something important. Paige came across some funny-looking rocks. These rocks had some funny-looking minerals on them, minerals that look like gold.

"Hey, guys, take a look at this. Do you think these rocks have real gold on them?" She was holding up the shiny rocks.

The boys glanced at each other, thinking the same thing. "We're going to be rich!" They all had dollar signs in their eyes.

Mark suggested that they collect all the gold rocks that they could find. They worked very hard collecting them. They hid the golden rocks in a nearby brush and disguised the area so that no one could find them.

They didn't even notice that it was almost suppertime and that it was getting pretty dark outside. They decided it was time to head home. After all, they felt like they were starved. Before they left, they made a pact not to breathe a word to anyone about the gold that they had found.

Alyssa began to walk down the first path that she came to. After a little while, she came to some train tracks. She looked both ways to see if any trains were coming. She knew that it was a bad idea to walk on the train tracks, but just then she thought, *Why not? It will be a lot quicker.* Her mom had always told her to stay off the train tracks, because you could get seriously injured. With that thought in mind, she began to wonder when the last train had gone by. She had not seen or heard any trains for over an hour or so. Alyssa turned around and glanced behind her, but she still saw nothing. She glanced in front of herself, but there was nothing there, either. *This is very strange*, she thought to herself. She bent down and placed her hands on the rail to feel for the vibrations, and she could feel a weak vibration coming from the rails. She stood up and surveyed the train tracks again. In the distance, she could see some smoke coming her way.

I'd better get off these tracks before I get seriously hurt, she reminded herself. She left the tracks and moved about a hundred feet away. She could feel the breeze coming off the train as it went whizzing past her. She stood there watching the giant machine hurtling by her.

As she watched the train go by, she started to wish that her pest of a brother was with her. *Jack would love to see this*, she thought to herself. She really didn't enjoy being alone for very long. Because she wasn't paying attention to where she was walking, Alyssa stumbled right into a snake pit.

There were so many snakes, both babies and huge ones. It looked like there were thousands of them. Alyssa started screeching at the top of her lungs. She was so loud that a nearby team of Boy Scouts could hear her in the distance. They were working on their nature merit badges. The boys raced over toward the screaming and to see what all the commotion is all about. They started to snicker when they saw Alyssa screaming and dancing around in a circle, snakes all around her.

"Need some assistance, miss?" One of the young boys asked after a few moments.

"Get these snakes away from me!" Alyssa screamed as loud as she could.

"Calm down! Calm down! Give us your hands." The boys were trying so hard not to laugh at her. Alyssa stretched her hand out and grabbed a boy's hand.

"Thanks!" She said, relieved.

"Would you like to join us, at our campsite?"

"Sure!" Alyssa followed the boys back to their campsite then. She joined in with the sing-along and with the making of "smokes," which involved placing marshmallows and chocolate chips between two graham crackers and melting it over the open fire. The time flew by quickly, and the boys started gathering their things together.

As the boys piled into the back of a pickup truck, they asked Alyssa if they could give her a lift anywhere. Alyssa was delighted to accept a ride to Smith Falls. The boys dropped her off at the Hershey plant.

It was early enough for Alyssa to join in the tour of the factory. She was fascinated with everything that she witnessed throughout the tour. The sweet smell of chocolates filtered through the air inside the chocolate factory. Alyssa felt like she was in heaven, for she just wanted to jump into the chocolate down below.

After the tour, Alyssa thought it would be great if she bought some baking goods. It would be great to have some of her favourite chocolates to take home with her. She loved to bake all kind of yummy stuff to eat. She always had fun in the kitchen with her mother, spending whole days in the kitchen and banking up a storm. She was thinking so much about the chocolate that she didn't see her godfather sneaking up behind her.

"Boo!" he said.

Alyssa screamed with fright and jumped three feet in the air. "You scared the heebie-jeebies out of me," she told her godfather, Rick, after she caught her breath.

"What are you doing here all by yourself, Alyssa?"

"I'm on my way to Ottawa to attend the hockey game tomorrow night."

"How about coming over to my place, visiting for a while, and having some supper with the family? We are having a family get-together. You can have a hot bubble bath, and we could possibly catch up with each other. I know my wife would love to see you again."

"That sounds splendid. Let's go," she responded with a smile.

Rick and Alyssa headed over to his place. After she entered the nice, comfortable home, Alyssa was soon relishing in a steaming hot bubble bath. She soaked in the hot water and blew on the bubbles for probably an hour. As she was leaving the bathroom, she bumped into Adam, Rick's two-year-old grandson.

Alyssa picked up Adam and began to tickle and dance with him. Adam was having so much fun that he started to giggle really hard, almost having a hysterical fit in the process. She then walked into the family room, where the rest of the family was sitting around and chatting about the good old days.

Soon, it was suppertime. Everyone proceeded into the dining room and sat down. The table was stuffed with all kinds of appetizing foods. There was pork roast, potatoes wedges with gravy, peas and carrots, and cream corn. Dessert consisted of chocolate cake and frozen wild berry yogurt. Everyone started to sink their teeth into the tasty deserts. Afterward, Alyssa helped out by lending a hand with cleaning up.

Jack took great pride in his ability to leapfrog over large mud puddles. Swish, splash, and all the way home he leapt. Jack climbed under the house and started digging up the stash of money that he had buried there. He had been saving his money for a very long time. He was earning money by doing jobs around the house for his mother and doing some odd jobs for some of the neighbours. He would help them out by cutting their lawns and washing their windows. As he held the money in his left hand, he started to count his savings. Thinking of his goal to purchase a video game system and the locomotive game that went with it the whole time.

Jack dreamed of becoming a train engineer someday. He spent most of his free time trying to discover and learn whatever he could about trains. One day, he would like to invent a train that would run off the energy of the sun, a train that used solar power. He believed in his heart that it would be one of the best things for the environment.

Jack really loved trying new things, and he had the ability to put things together in a way that no one else had ever imagined before. He felt that he was already a great inventor. The only problem was that he seemed to almost always end up getting into some type of trouble lately. To cause fewer problems for himself, he would take his ideas and theories and spend a couple of hours entering them into the computer.

"Wow!" He exclaimed, not believing his own eyes. "I've save up five hundred dollars. This is so cool. I didn't realize I had saved this much. I have enough money now that I can purchase the games that I want." As he thought to himself, he realized he could buy something fabulous for his mother and maybe a little gift for his sister, too.

Jack could hear his mother calling him for supper. He reburied his stash of money once more and climbed out from beneath the house. He raced around the corner of the house and tumbled right into another mud puddle. He then raced up the stairs into the living room, where his mother was placing some money on the counter for Zoë the baby-sitter.

Susan noticed that Zoë had made some cherry pies; however, when she went to thank Zoë for doing the baking, she noticed that Zoë had already left for home. Susan knew she could pay her later, so Susan picked up the phone to order an extra-large meat lover's pizza for supper.

She yelled out to the kids, but Alyssa was still exploring her dreamland. She glanced over at Jack and said, "Jack, you need to have another bath, dear. Hurry! I don't want all that mud all over my clean floors."

Jack did as he was told to do.

Susan sat down to work on a crossword puzzle, relaxing while she waited for the pizza to arrive. Soon, there was a knock at the front door, which could be heard throughout the house. After she walked over to the door, she opened it and paid the boy for the delicious-smelling pizza.

Jack flew down the stairs as soon as he heard the front doors open. Susan handed the pizza over to Jack and told him to be very carefully when he helped himself to a slice.

Susan walked upstairs and knocked on Alyssa's bedroom door. There was no response. She slowly opened the bedroom door, trying very hard not to startle her daughter. She glanced over at Alyssa just lying there as still as could be. She walked over to her and placed her hand on Alyssa's shoulder and gave her a little shake to snap her out of her daydream.

"Hi, sweetie, come down and have some pizza with us."

The two ladies headed downstairs and joined Jack in the dining room. They each grabbed a slice of pizza and a soda pop. They were all sitting around the table and eating when Jack started to tell a story about an old, shaggy dog. Then Susan started to tell them about an old Indian legend that was told to her when she was a little girl.

Even Alyssa joined in the fun by telling a few jokes that she had heard recently. Suddenly, they all were laughing so hard that they almost wet their pants. After they cleaned up the supper dishes, they all went into the living room to watch some movies. They watched a movie, and then they started to play some card games. They talked and took turns telling a couple more jokes throughout the night.

Before they called it a night, they had some of Zoë's famous cherry pie with some tiger stripe ice cream. The children then went down to the basement and grabbed their sleeping bags. Susan went into the kitchen and popped some buttery popcorn for their slumber party. Susan brought the popcorn into the living room and climbed into her sleeping bag, which rested between the two kids. Susan finally put in another movie that the children had picked out.

Soon, everyone was comfortable in their sleeping bags, full of buttery popcorn. They lay there very tired as the movie continued. Soon, however, everyone fell fast asleep.

Chapter Three

COAL MINES AND HOCKEY GAMES

It was a spring day that felt like a nice, warm summer day. It was one of those days where you felt like you didn't need to wear a jacket. Outside, the many birds were playing a beautiful tune. In the background, a soft wind was blowing, too. The trees were doing the dance of nature, their branches swaying back and forth.

Susan woke up and listened to the song of the outdoor through her window. She could tell it was going to be another gorgeous day. She always felt at peace when she could listen to nature sing its song. She quickly entered the bathroom to start her morning ritual of a warm shower. She tied up the bathroom for a long while.

Susan headed to the closest to get dressed for work. When she eventually headed downstairs, she poured herself a steaming cup of black coffee from the automatic coffee machine, which she had filled up the night before. Slowly waking up, she began to make some blueberry pancakes for the kids. With her cup of morning coffee in hand, she sat comfortably at the dining room table and waited for the children to wake up.

Jack sat up in his bed and tried to come up with a plot to get back at Alyssa for yesterday's stunt. *I've got it*, he thought. He slipped out of bed, quietly crept down to his mother's bathroom, and took her shaving cream. He crept back in his bedroom and took a feather from a wooden box that he had hidden in the closest. Softly, he tiptoed down to Alyssa's bedroom, where she was still fast asleep. He sprayed some shaving cream into her left hand and began tickling her nose with the feather.

Alyssa brought up her left hand and then splat! She hit herself right in the nose with a handful of shaving cream. "I'm going to kill you, Jack," she said. She jumped quickly out of her bed and chased Jack down the stairs right into the dining room, where their mother was quietly drinking her coffee.

"Enough! You guys! Alyssa, go clean that off your face."

Still in their pyjamas, the children picked up their plates brimming full of blueberry pancakes along with a glass of freshly squeezed orange juice. They then joined their mother at the dining room table.

"Well, good morning, children. What is up for today? Is there anything special going on today?"

"No, there is nothing special going on today," they both replied at the same time.

"Aw, come on, guys. It's mom here. There must be something going on."

"Okay! I'm going to fix my bike, and then if it's okay, I would like to go bike riding with Mark and Paige."

Alyssa just stared at her mother. After a few moments, she replied, "Well, I don't know. I'm thinking of going to my room again."

Susan just glanced at her daughter and began to wonder if she was depressed about something. For the past three days, all she had done was lie on her bed and stare off into space. Susan didn't have the time to think about this problem or come up with a solution to it right then, because she was running late for work once again.

"Why don't you call a friend over or arrange something with Zoë?" she suggested to Alyssa as she bent down and gave her a kiss on the forehead.

"No thanks! Mom I just want to relax and do my own thing and nothing else."

"Okay, it was just a suggestion. Well, behave. We'll discuss this later. I'm off to work."

Alyssa rolled her eyes and shook her head. She was just starting to clean up the breakfast dishes when Zoë walked into the dining room.

"Good morning, Alyssa. Was that your mother leaving for work? She is running late today."

"Yeah, that was her. Jack is outside in the garage working on his bike. Mom said he could go riding with Mark and Paige, or at least that's what I think he's doing anyway. I'm off to my room."

She climbed the stairs, taking them two at a time. She took a glimpse out of her bedroom window and wondered if her mother was right. Maybe she should call one of her friends from school and invite them over. It could be fun. Instead, she turned on some tunes and lay back down on her bed. After some time passed, she drifted back into her imagination.

Now where was I? She asked herself. *Oh yeah, I was at my godfather's place.*

"Well, I should be on my way," Alyssa said to her godfather.

"I don't think so! I have the perfect ideal. How about you and I go catch a glimpse of the game together? It can be a father-and-daughter date. It's been a long time since we did anything together, so how about it?"

Alyssa just stood there thinking. This wasn't in her plans. After a few moments passed, she decided that her godfather's suggestion could be fun. "Well, it's been a long time since we've done anything together. Sure, why not! Let's get going. It was time to head out anyway."

It was still early in the morning when they started out, heading toward Ottawa. Along the way, they saw a baby blue car pull over to the side of the road, with its hood up. There was some smoke coming from the car, and it was packed with people.

"Look at that!" Alyssa said and pointed out the car window. "Those people need our help. We shouldn't leave them stranded."

"You're right! It's not safe for people to be stranded alongside of the road anymore. We should offer our assistance to them and get them on their way."

To Alyssa's great surprise, it was some of the Gladiators' players. They were on their way to the same game just like Alyssa was.

Alyssa didn't know what to do. She just stood there like a statue for a few minutes while Rick assisted them with their car. Alyssa got up her nerve, went over, and started talking to some of the other players. She introduced herself and told them that she was a huge fan of their team. She then told them all about her going to see the hockey game; however, she stuttered all the way though her little speech to them.

The team's goalie then reached into the glove compartment and pulled out two VIP passes to the game. He handed them over to Alyssa and said it was his way in saying thank you to a huge fan for all their help. With these passes, she would be able to meet all the players on both hockey teams. It was like a dream come true. The team thanked them once again, and the Gladiators were once more on their way to Ottawa.

"Shall we get going, Alyssa?"

All excited, she responded, "Sure thing! Let's get going."

Along the way, they picked up a hitchhiker. She had short, brunette hair and hazel eyes. She stood about five foot five inches tall. She looked to be in her twenties, too. She was nervous and acted sheepish and apprehensive when she was in the car. She clung very tightly to a pink gym bag filled with her personal belongings like makeup, clothes, and some perfumes. She seemed like she wasn't capable of making eye contact for more than a moment .Alyssa offers her hand for comfort to the young lady. She took a hold of Alyssa hand so slightly that Alyssa could feel her trembling. Alyssa started to crack up some jokes and try to get the young lady to laugh. An hour went by quickly. They eventually dropped the young lady off at her destination. She never gave her name or said very much. She was a complete mystery.

"That was very strange," Alyssa stated as she glanced over to her godfather.

"We're almost there, and we are here earlier than I expected to be. Is there anything special you wish to do while we wait for the game to start?"

"We can go have some lunch, and maybe we could get in some shopping,

"Any place special you would be keen on going to?"

"We could go to the mall. Maybe we should go to the dinosaur place for lunch. It's been a long time since we went there."

They did a little shopping and grabbed a bite to eat and then started to head over to the hockey arena. They didn't have to purchase their tickets for the game. They had special tickets given to them from members of the Ottawa Gladiators. They settled down into their seats and waited for the exciting game between the Gladiators against the Toronto team to start.

It was an outstanding game. The score was very close one, the score 5–4, the Gladiators winning in the end. There were a few fistfights and lots of penalties for both teams. Alyssa could tell that neither team really liked each other. At halftime, Alyssa dashed down to the souvenir counter to purchase a jacket, a hat, gloves, and even a book bag, all with the Gladiators' logo on them.

Afterward, Alyssa and Rick made for the locker room, where they greeted all the players from both hockey teams. Alyssa received everyone's autograph. She told them all that it had been an exceptional game. She thanked them all for signing their names in her book and said good-bye to them. In all her wildest dreams, she had never thought something like this could have ever happened to her.

Alyssa was so excited about the game that she couldn't stop chatting up a storm. She talked nonstop about the game. She wished that it would have never ended. She chatted with Rick until they stopped for another bite to eat. After they ate, they continued on their way back to Rick's house. They told some stories and a few jokes along the way.

Before she left Rick's, she grabbed a snack and a drink. She thanked Rick for the wonderful time that she had had with him. She collected her things and then gave her godparents a hug and a kiss good-bye. She told them not to worry and that she would be fine. As she ran out the door, she shouted, "Good-bye." She headed down the road toward the way home.

Jack slipped on his clothes and went into the garage, where his bike was parked. He started to examine his bike then. He eventually decided to rearrange the handlebars so they stood up straight. Next, he adjusted the seat so that it was more comfortable when he was out riding or going over bumps and hills. He repaired the spokes so they were straight, and he twisted the mirror so he could catch a glimpse of things behind him when he was out riding.

"That's everything! Off I go," he said. He opened the garage door and hopped onto his bike and away he went. The first person he bumped into was Mark. The boys rode around for a while and made a decision to go down to the train tracks and investigate the area. The boys settled on going north down the tracks. They had never checked out that part of the tracks before.

They stopped for a minute. They stared at a dark black hole that was deep in a mountaintop. The boys parked their bikes against the mountain. This hole seemed to be an old coal mine. This would make a cool hideout. The boys walked over to the front entrance, peeked in, and gathered up their nerve as they slowly went inside. Shortly after they entered the colliery, Jack tripped over a box of food. What the heck was that doing here? As they advanced deeper into the dark hole, the boys looked around and finally came across some helmets with lights on them. The boys put the helmets on their heads and turned on the lights and began to look around them. To their surprise, they came across a heap of blankets and toys. They even saw some shovels and axes. This didn't make any sense to them, because there was no one in sight. No noise came out of the tunnel. It was unusually quiet. Where was everyone? The boys started to feel unsure about what was happening. The boys traveled a little farther into the mysterious tunnel, using the lights of the helmets. Suddenly, they came to a halt. There, right in front of them, was an old coal car.

"There must be gold in here. Let's go back and get Paige. She would love to catch a glimpse of this," Mark replied.

"Yeah, right, Paige would appreciate something like this," Jack agreed.

The boys quickly left the coal mine tunnel and then proceeded to Paige's residence. Her mother told them that Paige was out fooling around somewhere. The boys looked mystified, because Paige was always with one of them. They started to speculate about where she might have been. The boys contemplated this question for a little while, trying to figure out where she might be hanging out.

"I know where she might be!" Jack said.

"Where do you think she might be?" Mark asked.

"What about the library? We were working on some research for a project that we are doing together."

The boys traveled over to the library, but they didn't stumble across her there, either.

"What about the recreational area. You know how she enjoys clowning around with the little kids," Mark suggested.

But Paige wasn't there, either. Where could she have gone? They talked it over with each other, trying to figure out an answer. They rode around the neighbourhood for a while and searched for their friend. They finally found Paige near the pile of gold, which they had laid there the day before. The boys immediately rode over to Paige. They were exhausted, so they decided to get off their bikes and sit underneath a maple tree. Once they had caught their breath, they informed her about the coal mine that they had discovered. Soon, the three buddies were on their bikes heading back to the coal mine. They stopped out front and parked their bikes beside the mountain.

"Wait, you guys! How extensively are we going to investigate? This could be very dangerous. We might get injured, you know. We should consider everything before we proceed."

"Stop being such a girl, Paige," the boys hollered back.

The three friends began to follow the tracks down past the coal car, and each of them reached down to grab a helmet and an axe. They stumbled down the old tunnel for almost a mile, not paying much attention to where they were walking. All of a sudden, they heard a crash. Paige had tumbled down a gap in the floor into an old mine shaft.

"Help with me," her voice rang from the hole in the tunnel.

The boys attempted to help Paige, but they just couldn't reach her. Jack told her to stay calm until they could figure out some way of getting her out of the gaping hole. The boys searched around them to see if there was anything that they could use to help their friend out. A big zilch was all they found—in other words, they found nothing.

Jack thought for a moment, trying to come up with a plan. "I've got it. Mark, you can lower me down to her and heave us up, provided that I can reach her." This was going to be quite a challenge for them. Mark clutched Jack's ankles and gradually lowered him down to where Paige was waiting patiently. Suddenly, Mark lost his grip, and he was pulled into the hole along with his friend. Both of them landed right on top of Paige.

"Are you okay, Paige? I didn't mean to drop Jack and myself on you."

Paige and Jack started whispering to each other, wondering what to do next. Jack reminded Mark and Paige that they should all stick together.

"Hey! There appears to be some light down the tunnel," Paige stated.

"We should check it out," Jack suggested.

"Yeah, let's check it out. What do we have to lose?" Agree Mark and Paige

The three buddies crawled slowly down the tight, narrow passageway. They had to crawl along the ground, and slowly, they head toward the light. Naturally, it was very scary. They were all unsure about what was waiting for them up ahead. Paige confessed to the boys that she was frightened, and the boys agreed that they were also scared. They would only admit it to each other, not to a girl, friend or no friend.

To their surprise, when they finally arrived at the light, they caught sight of twenty to thirty people huddled together in a circle. Some of them were weeping. Some were humming tunes to themselves, and some of them looked completely lost with fright. Not one of them knew what to do. The people were barely just surviving in this dark tunnel away from the world. It turned out that they had been trying for who knew how long to figure out a way to get back to the first floor and back to their belongings. The three buddies looked shocked for a moment as they realized that they had found a group of missing people. Paige, Mark, and Jack stood up and started to wipe the grime off their clothes.

They walked over and greeted the group of people. One of the elder approached the kids and said, "Are we glad to catch sight of you! How on earth did you come across us? We were working down here when the wall collapse on us we've been trying to dig owner self out. We've search everywhere and came up empty for two days now. We have no cell phone reception down here so we couldn't call for help that way and we have very little water left with us."

Do you think you might be able to show us a way out of here? We would be forever grateful to you three."

The three buddies started to whisper to each other, but they couldn't come up with a single idea. Jack started to draw a map on the soil floor. It was the only way that he might be able to formulate any kind of plan. After a few moments passed, a brainstorm filled his mind.

"I've got it! We all could crawl back to where the three of us fell in. Then we can climb on top of each other's shoulders. Maybe some of you stronger men can pull some of us all up."

"That's a terrific ideal. Why didn't any of us think of that?" the elder said.

One by one, they crawled back down the tight passageway and eventually reached the opening, where the three youngsters had fallen though. Two of the men who were physically powerful climbed out first. Quickly, they started to pull the others out one at a time. They all headed toward the front entrance, where all their belongings had been left.

The elder in the group started up a blazing fire for everyone. They all joined in the celebration of being free once again. They sat around the campfire to keep warm. They all told stories about the old pioneer who had once lived in the colliery back in the days. They told a few funny stories that got everyone laughing. Before long, it was time for Jack and friends to head home, because it was getting late. Everyone in the coal mine thanked their new friends for all their help. As a gift, they gave them each a small ruby to take home with them. Farewells were yelled out to them.

Jack and his friends had never known anyone who celebrated life to the fullness. They put their rubies in their pocket and then hopped on their bikes, and away they went.

Meanwhile, without any hesitation, Alyssa was on her way home. She came across a narrow pathway that she had never noticed before. She decided to follow the pathway though the woods. *Quite spooky out here*, thought Alyssa, beginning to get scared. Alyssa began to quiver as she went farther into the woods.

Suddenly, she heard something out of the ordinary. She couldn't distinguish what it was. She had never experienced this kind of sound before. It sounded like some kind of hurt animal. She just couldn't figure it out. She began to wonder what kind of creature could make such a horrifying sound.

She saw many different kinds of animals in the forest. There were chipmunks racing and running around the trees and squirrels hiding their nuts. There were many different kinds of birds chirping cheerfully. There was even a family of red foxes sleeping in a den nearby.

Alyssa sat down to take a tiny break, for her legs were starting to get tried from all the walking she had done. She eventually gathered up some small pieces of wood. Soon, she had a noisy fire going, gleaming brightly. Still scared, she pulled out a ham-and-cheese sandwich. Hungry, she started to take a bite.

As she looked at her surroundings, she glanced up at one of the high pine trees. She caught sight of a pair of red eyes staring right at her. What *kind of creature has red eyes?* She began to wonder. She screamed loudly as the creature approached her. Alyssa sat low to the ground, quivering with fright. She didn't move an inch as the creature come closer to her. Whatever this was, it sat down beside the fire to get warm and then took a quick glance at Alyssa.

She had never come across anything like this before. What kind of creature was this? Alyssa didn't know what to do. This creature was about four feet tall, and it had long bluish black hair, with deep red eyes. Its hands and feet were webbed like a duck's feet. Its ears were huge like an elephant's. Its nose was six inches long, too. Alyssa just stared at it, unsure of what it might do to her.

"You know it's not polite to stare."

It spoke! This flabbergasted Alyssa, for animals didn't usually talk. What was this? "Oh, I'm sorry," she said, stammering. "I didn't mean to stare."

After some time had passed and the uneasiness went away, the creature asked Alyssa if she minded that she sat near the fire to keep warm with her.

"Yes, please do. What is your name?"

"I really don't know! It's been a long time since anyone has talked to me or called me by name."

"Well, how about Jenny? You look like a Jenny to me."

Because she felt very awkward, Alyssa decided to question Jenny about why she looked the way she did. "Well, how come you look the way you do?"

Jenny replied with a chuckle, "Well, to tell you the truth, I was an experiment that went wrong. I was born and raised in the Black Diamond Circus. People would come from miles and miles just to stare, point, and laugh at me. I didn't enjoy that, so I scampered away but before doing so I overheard the doctors say that I had a twin brother name Carlos. I've been here ever since then. I just want to be like everyone else. I guess that will never happen. Just look at me. I'm not exactly what you would call normal!"

"What is normal nowadays?" Alyssa said and began to giggle. "There isn't one perfect person in the world. What they did to you was extremely wrong. Everybody is special in their own tiny way. That's what makes us all unique. If everybody was the same or perfect, it would make it a boring world. Don't you agree? Besides that, there are doctors out there that can be of assistance to you, and maybe they could help you, Jenny."

"Really? There doctors out there that could help me appear normal?" This was music to Jenny's ears, for she had wished this her whole life.

"Yes, actually, there are."

Jenny made a decision that she would demonstrate a few of her special abilities to Alyssa. She picked up Alyssa and flew up into the beautiful blue sky above. Jenny could fly! Up they went, flying over a nearby lake. Alyssa covered her eyes, only taking an occasional peek through her fingers. She could see the lake sparkling like a midnight star. They flew over a school yard where some children were out playing Double Dutch and basketball on the court. They soared fast, twisting and turning. They soared over some nearby buildings and headed back toward the forest.

"Wow, that was amazing," Alyssa reported as she tried to catch her breath. "I could never do something like flying. People just can't do that. It's not normal. You have a very special gift here. Why would you ever want to get rid of such a wonderful gift? I wish I could fly, for everything appears so beautiful and so tiny."

The ladies headed down to the lake in the vicinity. Alyssa took off her socks and her running shoes and began to soak her feet in the cold water. Jenny told Alyssa to wait there while she went fishing for the two of them. She was back in a flash, with a couple of catfish for them to eat.

Alyssa was flabbergasted by everything Jenny had achieved. She soon realized that she couldn't do half the things Jenny could. Alyssa wondered why other people couldn't see the amazing things that Jenny could do or get the message that we were all different. Instead, they just laughed at her, which was heartbreaking to know. She didn't realize that people could be so vindictive.

The two ladies enjoyed their fish with some fish eggs. Jenny started to paint a better picture of what life was really like for her. She eventually said that a team of doctors had this brilliant idea that they could create the perfect person. They tried to create a person who could do everything and anything without needing any assistance to learn. *Wishful thinking on their part!* Alyssa thought.

Jenny let out a tiny chuckle. "As you can see, it backfired on them, and they ended up with me instead. They didn't want me, so they sold me to the circus. I got tired of people pointing and laughing at me, so I dashed out of there as fast as I could. I know I'm repeating myself again, but sometimes I do that." After a pause, Jenny continued, "So what is your story, Alyssa? You're out here all by yourself?"

Alyssa was trying to figure that out herself. She wondered if she could live like Jenny. *Probably not*, she told herself. As far as she knew, she was curled up on her bed, sleeping. Alyssa shook her head. She wasn't sure what was going on. She knew she could never have lived a life similar to Jenny's or have done half of the things Jenny had accomplished.

"Oh, I went to a hockey game, and now I'm heading home. Would you be keen on coming to my place? You could see what a real family is like. My mom could probably lend you a hand with any problems that you may have. Not that you need any assistance with anything."

In spite of everything Jenny had lived through, she was still unsure on how things would work out, because she was abnormal to everyone else. The two ladies curled up next to the campfire and fell fast asleep.

Jack, Mark, and Paige decided that it was getting late, so they said farewell to their new friends. Then they started to travel down the train tracks and head back home.

When Jack came close to his bungalow, he could smell the roses and pine trees and all the beautiful fragrances coming from the kitchen. The table was beautifully set. It was like he had walked into a fantasy world, a place where dreamers were welcome. It had been a very long time since they had all sat at the table together like this. There were flowers in the center of the table, too. Place mats were set at every spot. Silverware was in its proper place. Jack began to wonder what was up.

"Mom, I'm home," he called. "Where are you?"

But there was no response.

Jack began to search the house, going from room to room until he found her sitting in front of the computer and working. Jack walked upstairs to check on everything, but it was the same as before. He poked his head through his sisters' bedroom door. *This is very strange*, he thought to himself. Jack walked toward his sister. Something just wasn't right here. He then noticed that Alyssa was sweating badly.

"Mom, Mom, come quick! It's sissy. I think she is really sick," yelled Jack.

Susan raced up the stairs, taking them two at a time, until she reached Alyssa's bedroom. She took Alyssa's temperature using a thermometer from the bathroom. She asked Jack to grab a couple of wet compresses so that she could try to bring down her daughter's fever. Jack handed her an ice-cold compress soon after that. Susan took the compress from Jack and showed him where to hold it on his sister's face. Quickly, she phoned the doctor to see if he could make a house call.

Susan picked Alyssa up and carried her down to the living room. She gently laid her down on the couch. Susan then wiped Alyssa's forehead down with the cold compress. Susan then got some medicine for Alyssa to help bring down the fever, and she even made sure her daughter swallowed the pills.

Susan went into the kitchen and dished out some chilli in two bowls for her and Jack. She then made up some chicken soup for Alyssa while she waited nervously for the doctor to show up.

After Jack put the dishes in the dishwasher, he went upstairs to his room to study his notes for his invention. He started to toss his toys around the room. He was searching for a broken train that he knew he had. "Aw, found it," he eventually said. He then looked around the room at the mess he had just made and continued "I'll clean this up tomorrow before mom sees it."

Meanwhile, Susan tried to feed Alyssa some chicken soup. She sat very close to Alyssa to keep a close eye on her while she nervously read a report from the office. Everything was as quiet as a mouse, Jack studying his notes and trying to fix his broken train. Susan reading and watching over her daughter.

A gentle rain started to fall. Alyssa and Jenny were starting to get wet, but they were determined to stay dry. Naturally, they started to make a shelter. The ladies grabbed some tree branches to make a hut. The ladies talked and laughed throughout the night. They told ghost stories, and Alyssa continued telling Jenny what it was like to have a family, how her baby brother, Jack, could be a real pain in the butt but how she loved him like an adorable puppy at the same time. She also told Jenny what it was like having a loving mother who was always around when she needed her.

"Sound great to me! Do you think I could have a family like that someday?"

"Sure, why not?" Alyssa said.

Jack began to feel really tired, and soon, he was fast asleep, his arm draped over his broken train set. Susan took a break to see how Jack was doing. She carried him up to his room and laid him down on his bed. She glanced around the room and gave her head a little shake. *Well, I guess Jack will clean his room first thing in the morning,* Susan thought to herself.

Susan then heard someone knocking at the front door. As she looked through the tiny peephole in the front door, she noticed that it was the doctor and immediately let him in the house.

"Hi, Doctor Axle, the patient is in the living room."

"Ah, let's see what we have here. Oh! Ah," he stated with a puzzled look on his face. "I really don't know what is wrong. I'll take a blood sample and go back to the lab. I'll see if anything shows up in the blood work. Keep an eye on her for now and call me if there is any change. She could just have the 24hr flu. Give her plenty of liquid and rest and call me in the morning if anything changes. "

"Thanks for coming over so quickly. I'll phone if there are any changes."

Doctor Axle gave Susan some instructions for her daughter's care when he left. "I'll talk to you later then. Bye!"

Susan checked on Jack and then grabbed a blanket and curled up at the other end of the couch, where Alyssa was fast asleep. Susan watched her daughter and wondered if her little girl was coming down with something. *Maybe it has something to do with all the sleeping she's done over the last few days,* Susan then thought.

Chapter Four

RAINBOWS AND OLD WIVES' TALES

When Alyssa woke, she could smell the aroma of fresh rain lingering in the air. She had always loved the smell of fresh rain. She glanced over to where Jenny was fast asleep. *I ought to see if I am able to find something for the two of us to munch on for breakfast,* she thought.

Alyssa left the little hut that Jenny and she had prepared. In the sky, there was a beautiful rainbow unlike anything she had ever seen before, the beautiful colors blending together in the blue sky. Alyssa started to wonder if there was such a thing as a pot of gold at the end of the rainbow. Everybody seemed to believe in the old wives' tale that there was a pot of gold at the end of the rainbow. *It would be great if I could prove without a doubt that there is a pot of gold at the end of the rainbow,* she thought, *but how can I find out for sure and provide the evidence that there is such a thing?*

Alyssa came across some fresh blueberries and began to pick them as she pondered how she could find out the truth about the stories she had heard about gold at the end of rainbows. Alyssa continued picking the berries until she had filled the bucket. When she was back at the tiny hut, she noticed that Jenny was starting to stir.

Alyssa eventually pitched the idea of a pot of gold at the end of the rainbow to Jenny. They would be rich if it were true. What would they do with all that gold? Jenny just glared at Alyssa for a moment as she took another handful of blueberries. "I actually don't know. Why do you want to know? There is a small possibility that we could look into the whole idea if you are really keen on finding out the truth, Alyssa."

"How on earth could we ever discover the truth about the pot of gold? No one knows how to retrieve it or what end that it sits at."

Jenny picked up Alyssa, and up she flew into the sky. "We could fly there to each end of the rainbow and discover the truth." Jenny flew right into the beautiful colors of the rainbow. Alyssa was so surprised. She never imagined that she would someday be able to touch the colors of the rainbow with her hands. Jenny started to do some tricks again, which made Alyssa a little sick to her stomach.

"This is fun and scary at the same time," Alyssa hollered out between moments of dizziness.

"Do you really want to know the answer to your question, Alyssa?"

"Yeah, I really would like to know if the old wives' tale is true or not."

"Hey, wake up, Mom. You're going to be late for work again. Zoë is already here."

Jack had already put on a pot of coffee for his mom. He had even made breakfast for both of them. Jack put down some orange juice and poured some cereal into two bowls.

"Thank, honey, but I could have done this."

"Mom, I'm old enough to do this on my own, you know. I'm not a baby anymore, you know."

"I know, but sometimes moms need a little reminder every now and then. We sometimes forget that our children are not 'babies' anymore."

Susan finished her breakfast and put the dirty dishes in the dishwasher. She then proceeded to get dressed for work. She gave Zoë some instructions to watch for changes in Alyssa's condition. She then gave the kids a hug and a kiss good-bye. She asked Jack to give Zoë any help she needed when she was dealing with his sister.

Jack escaped to his bedroom to clean up his mess from yesterday's search for the broken train. After he was done, he went into the living room to check on his big sis. He checked her over to make sure there was no change yet in her condition as he had promised his mom.

He dug out his coat and boots. *Now I'm ready to start today's adventure with my friends*, he thought. He really didn't know what today's grand adventure was going to be or even what might happen. When he walked over to the front door, a surprise hit him. *Swish!*—a gust of wind whizzed past him, knocking him over backward.

"What in the world was that?" Jack remarked as he was getting up.

Zoë rushed over quickly to see what had happened. "Are you okay?" she asked Jack as she pulled him up with a helping hand.

"Yeah, I'm fine," he said as he wiped down his pants. "Thanks. What was that anyway?"

"It looks like a small tornado is coming down our way. I think that it might be a good idea if you stay inside today, Jack. Why don't you invite a couple of your friends over instead? It might be a good idea if you did it soon before the storm gets any worst."

"Okay! This is going to be great!" Jack went over to the phone and invited his two best friends over. "They are on their way!" Jack hollered. Then he started getting things ready before his friends arrived. He looked for some board games. He got his notes and the broken train so that they could work on their invention together. Last thing he did before his friends arrived was grab some refreshments. He took everything into the den. Paige was the first to arrive at the house. She was soaked to the bone. Zoë handed her a towel to dry off with. The two friends then proceeded into the den. They each grabbed some notes that were starting to get crumpled up and began to go over them. Both of them started to drift into a daydream about their train that could run off solar power. Their heads were leaning against each other.

As the two friends were daydreaming, their friend Mark finally arrived. Mark took off his raincoat. He leaned it up against the wall to dry as he yanked off his boots. Zoë told him that the other two were in the den. As he stood at the den doorway, Mark started to chuckle out loud. "You two look so sweet there with your heads together like that. People will be saying that you two are sweethearts." Mark teased his two best friends.

"Knock it off, Mark! You know we are just friends. We are thinking if you want to join us, okay. If not, go home! We have worked to do," they responded.

Mark glanced at his friends with a confused expression on his face. "Working on what? What have you two been working on without me?" Mark questioned, feeling a little left out. The two friends brought Mark up to speed on what they had been working on for the last couple of days. They showed him illustration on what they had already done and what they would like to accomplish.

Mark was not impressed, his friends leaving him in the dark about what they had been up to! "Well, I want to help, too!"

They went through their notes with Mark. They all looked over the broken train. They decided to let Mark work on the train and see if he could somehow fix it. Mark was excellent at fixing things, and they all knew it. Mark was kind of a genius when it came to repairing things.

Paige was good at anything she tried, so she was willing to work on the rough drawing that would map out their process, even covering how the train should look when they were ready to take it for a the test drive.

Jack excelled when it came to taking notes. He would work on the notes and make sure they had everything that was needed.

The children worked on their individual projects all morning long. As she kept an eye on all four kids, Zoë started to make lunch. She decided on making some mushroom soup with ham-and-cheese sandwiches for everyone to munch on.

"Kids, it is lunchtime. Come and get it," Zoë hollered.

The three children hurried and finished up what they were working on at that very moment. "We can finish this after lunch," Jack told his friends.

The three of them joined Zoë in the kitchen. They grabbed their lunch and carried it into the dining room. They quickly sat down and started enjoying the soup and sandwiches. Then they all carried their dirty dishes and put them in the dishwasher.

Then they once again headed back into the den to work on their individual projects.

Zoë continued putting a cold compress on Alyssa's forehead. She attempted to feed Alyssa some soup. Alyssa was still feeling very weak and only took a few sips of the soup. After all, mushroom soup was her favorite soup. "That's it. Keep this up, and you'll be strong in no time. You'll see," Zoë informed Alyssa.

Alyssa eventually drifted back into her daydream. *Now where was I?* She thought. *Oh yeah, I was flying up in the sky with Jenny.* The girls were determined to find out the truth about the pot of gold at the end of the rainbow. Alyssa guaranteed Jenny that if she continued to do all those flying tricks; she was going to throw up all over the place. Jenny gave Alyssa a sideways look and then said, "Very well. I was trying to have some fun, you know. Well, let's get started on searching for that pot of gold."

First, they turned to the left of the rainbow, but nothing was there. Then they went right, and before they reached the other end, the rainbow disappeared. "We'll have to try again someday to find out the truth." Alyssa replied.

Jenny circled around the baby blue sky, Alyssa admiring the view. "Hey, take a peek down there! Want to go swimming in that ravine over there?" Jenny asked.

"Sure! Why not! But we don't have our bathing suits with us."

"We don't need our swimwear. No one is going to be around within miles of here. No one will ever catch a glimpse of us out here. It will be okay."

Alyssa was unsure of what to do. "I guess it will be all right."

Jenny flew down to the ravine. The ladies searched carefully around them to make sure that no one was nearby. The ladies then started to take their clothes off piece by piece. They didn't want their clothes to get soaked. They jumped into the freezing water, which felt wonderful to the touch on a hot spring day.

The ladies splashed around in the ravine, but they didn't know that there was a pair of eyes watching them as they splashed around in the cool water.

Jenny stopped swimming. She was getting a weird feeling that they were no longer alone at the ravine. She glanced around the ravine to see if there was anyone watching them. She didn't want to say anything to Alyssa. After all, it had been her idea to go swimming. She had been the one who had reassured Alyssa that it would be safe, but she just couldn't shake this awkward feeling of being watched. She wasn't exactly sure about it. Maybe it was just one of those weird moments. She didn't want to scare Alyssa, even though she could feel the eyes getting closer to them. She eventually just went back to swimming and having fun with Alyssa.

The pair of eyes left for a moment. The two eyes blinked, and a figure shuffled through the brushes back to his parents. He reported to his parents that there was a girl around his age at the ravine, one who looked identical to him, which he thought was very strange. After all, he had birth defects. His parents had to check it out for themselves. He couldn't understand how anyone could look exactly like him, because everyone he knew laughed at him or was afraid of him because of his birth defects.

This was why he always went to the ravine, because he wanted to be by himself most of the time. Sometimes he came there with his younger brother but no one else. He never imagined that he would be able to make friends around his own age, even though he secretly wished he could.

The two ladies splashed and swam around happily as the family tiptoed quietly over to the ravine to take a sneak peek at them.

"See what I'm implying? It's very peculiar, isn't it?"

Could this even be possible? How on earth could a girl look exactly like Carlos with all his deformity? Carlos's parents wondered. "Carlos! Why don't you go and greet the girls and see if they would like to come up to the house?"

Carlos just glared at his parents, scared of what they were suggesting. He just stood there, stunned, too afraid to even move. Every time he had tried to make a friend in the past, it had almost always ended up with them teasing him simply because of the way he looked.

His eyes and nose were a tiny bit bigger than normal. His hands and feet were webbed. Carlos didn't enjoy being teased, so he tried to stay away from people. Still unsure of what the ladies would think of him, Carlos slowly but steadily crept toward the ladies.

Jenny splashed around with Alyssa, going under the water and just having fun for once in her life with a true friend. She stopped splashing once again, and so did Alyssa.

"What is it, Jenny?"

"I don't know! I'm getting a feeling that someone is watching us."

"Well, I don't see or hear anyone. Let's go back to swimming and having fun, okay? You have nothing to be worry about. Just relax."

Carlos tiptoed even closer to them, and then he came out of his hiding spot.

"Hi, there, I'm Carlos."

The ladies glanced at each other and ducked under the water to hide from Carlos, but they were unable to hold their breath. They eventually popped their heads up out of the water.

"What on earth do you want?" the ladies shouted.

Carlos was about to leave when they asked. He thought for sure that this was going to be like all the other times when he had tried to make a friend. As he started to walk away, he took a sneak peep once again at the little girl who was around his age — or at least he guessed she was around his age — and saw how much alike they looked.

"My name is Carlos. I was just wondering if you ladies would like to hang out with me. I don't get to play with kids my age very often."

The young ladies looked at each and shrugged their shoulders. "Sure, why not! The more friends there are, the merrier we all shall be. But first, could you leave, Carlos, so we can get out of the water and get dressed?"

As he became more excited, Carlos stumbled over his words. "Oh! Yeah! It's a sure thing." As he grinned, Carlos turned his back to the girls so they could dress.

The girls slowly crept out of the water, unsure if they could trust Carlos, who might turn around and take a quick peek. They hurried as fast as they could get dressed. The girls sneaked up behind Carlos and yelled, "We're finished!"

Carlos jumped two feet in the air with fright. The girls started to laugh.

"Why on earth would you guys do that?"

"We thought it would be funny to see you jump."

Jenny and Carlos started to check each other out. This was amazing. They could almost pass as twins. That couldn't be possible—nor could it?

Alyssa started to wonder. As she listened to the two of them talk, Alyssa could not help but notice the similarities that her two new friends had. She started to think back to when she first met Jenny and what Jenny had told her about her life. Could it have been possible that these two were relate somehow?

Carlos asked the girls if they wanted to go to this place and meet his family. Alyssa thought this would be perfect, for they could find out for sure if Carlos and Jenny were related somehow. Then Jenny would have a family after all.

Jenny, on the other hand, had reservations about the hold idea. The last time she had been around a group of people, they had just laughed at her, and she didn't want to go through that again.

Alyssa could see that her friend was very afraid of the idea. She walked over to Jenny and whispered in her ear and placed her arm around Jenny's shoulder. "Everything is going to be all right. This could be the answers you've been waiting for. Think about it. You might have a family after all, and there's only one way to find out the truth."

Alyssa called Carlos over to where the two girls were talking. Alyssa spoke over Carlos's shoulders and said, "Sure, sound like a lot of fun. Lead the way."

Jack strolled into the den and started to polish up his notes, making sure that they would have everything that was need to make the train fully functional. Mark started restoring the broken train, making sure that it would work for the experiment, which they were all now working on.

Paige went back to drawing up the plans that they would follow throughout their experiment.

After a couple of hours had passed, the trio decided to take a break and started to play some games on the computer. Each of them took turns with the computer controls so that it would be fair.

The three were having so much fun that they didn't even notice the time flying by. Who would have reckoned that you could still find some interesting things to do even on a stormy day?

Zoë washed Alyssa with the cold compress once again, trying to bring down the high fever that she had. Afterward, she began to clean up the mess in the dining room. After she finished in the dining room, she started searching for the three kids, who were no longer in the den. After she walked from room to room, she finally stopped at the computer room. She stood there, leaning against the wall, watching the trio play quietly on the computer. Finally, she asked them if they would like to do some baking.

The trio glanced at each other with excitement. "Sure thing!" they said. Quickly, they closed up the game and shut off the computer. They then raced into the kitchen to begin the baking. *What are we going to bake?* They all wondered.

Zoë stopped for a moment. She just realized that everything was going very smoothly for once and started to wonder if there were any hidden surprises in store for her. Days like today never happened, so she began to wonder if a storm was brewing between the children. Zoë had a feeling that the children could have been cooking up some jokes to play on her.

The trio started to flip thought the cookbooks. They were having a hard time determining what to bake. As they flipped through the cookbook, Paige finally stopped at feather squares.

"What about feather squares?" she asked.

"Well, that's a funny name. What is it?" the boys inquired.

"It's Jell-O with cookie crumbs."

"Oh, okay," the boys said as they continued to flip though the cookbook. "What about zucchini bread?" they then asked.

"Okay, it sounds like the three of you have decided on what we are all going to make. Let's get started."

As the four of them baked up a storm in the kitchen, Susan arrived home from work. "Yummy! Something sure smell good in here! I must be in the wrong house," she joked as she walked into the kitchen.

"Mom, go away. We are busy here," ordered Jack.

"Oh! I'm sorry, honey. Mom can leave if you wish."

Susan left the kitchen and went into the living room to check on Alyssa. She wanted to see how her beautiful little princess was doing. As Susan moved closer to Alyssa, she could see that Alyssa was tossing and turning again.

"Oh! You're awake! How are you feeling?"

"I am tried and hot, Mom."

Susan went upstairs to run a cool bath for Alyssa. She then came back downstairs to help Alyssa up to the bathtub. When she proceeded downstairs, however, she stopped and poked her head into the kitchen to see what was going on. She just shook her head. "What a mess in here. It looks like you guys are having fun. Don't forget to clean up afterward," she reminded her little chefs.

"Okay, Mom. We get the message. Leave us alone now."

Susan thought she should phone Paige and Mark's parents to see if they could spend the night. Afterward, she went into the basement to look for the sleeping bags. Next, she took out some broad games that the children had in the cupboard. She brought out the games Sorry, Snakes and Ladders, Checkers and lots more. Last but not least, she took out some of their favorite movies to watch.

Susan then decided to order some supper. *Now what should I order?* She thought. *Let me think. Hmm!* She didn't want pizza again. She decided on poutine, some zucchini sticks with garlic sauce and some donairs with cheese and hot sauce for everyone. She quickly called Tasty Sauce Pizzeria and placed her order.

Susan then went upstairs once more to check on Alyssa and see how her daughter was doing. She grabbed her notes from the office and began to work on them while she waited for their supper to arrive.

Her little chefs eventually came out of the kitchen with example of their baking goods for her to try.

"This is excellent!" she said.

She then asked her little chefs if they had clean up their mess.

"Yes, we did," they said.

Susan answered the door and paid for the food. After she carried the food to the dining room, she asked her little chefs to grab the forks, knives, spoons, and some plates for supper. As they ate, Susan told Paige and Mark that they were spending the night.

After they cleaned up supper, Susan set the kids up with the broad games and told them to play quietly and fairly without fighting.

While the kids took turns playing the many broad games, Susan went back to her work.

Around 9:00 p.m., Susan told the kids to clean up the den. Afterward, they all climbed into their sleeping bags, which Susan had already laid out for them. Susan then put in the movie she had picked out for them to watch. Then she went into the kitchen and popped some popcorn in the microwave oven.

After she got the children settled in, Susan slipped into her pajamas. Then she grabbed a blanket and snuggled closely beside Alyssa on the couch.

Everyone was soon fast asleep.

Chapter Five

TWINS AND ALLIGATOR HUNGER

The children were up bright and early at the first break of dawn. They watched quietly as the sun rose over the mountain to start another day. They were all wondering what they were going to do for some excitement today. One thing was for sure—Jack was going to Playland Express to purchase the video game console and locomotive game that he wanted. He also wanted to see a jeweler about having his ruby turned into a pair of earrings and a necklace for his mom for Mother's Day. And maybe he would buy something small for his big sis.

Alyssa, on the other hand, just proceeded to her room once again.

Paige and Mark phoned home to get permission to go with Jack to Playland Express.

The kids started to jump and holler all around Susan in order to wake her up and let her know that they all were up, too. The kids picked up their sleeping bags and their pillows and put them away in the downstairs closest. Then they all proceeded upstairs to get dressed for the day.

Susan treaded lightly across the kitchen floor and instinctively turned on her coffee pot. She then took out some eggs, bacon, sausages, milk, and bread. Susan started cooking two sunny-sides up eggs, two scramble eggs, and ten pieces of toasts. She then cooked the bacon and sausages and poured five glasses of freshly squeezed orange juice.

"Come and get it," she hollered to the children as she poured a cup of coffee, reached for the plate of toast, and sat down at the dining room table. One by one, the children joined her with their breakfast and their orange juice. As everyone enjoyed their breakfast, Susan inquired about what they all had planned for the day. Afterward, she reminded them that she was going to be home early from work that day.

The children played in the den for a while. Susan went upstairs to take another shower and got dressed for work. She then grabbed her briefcase and quickly ran out the door. She yelled out, "Be good."

Zoë reached the door while Susan went flying by. With Susan off to work, Zoë just stood there, scratching her head, wondering what she was going to do with four kids today. Luckily, she had brought her goody bag with her. Maybe, just maybe she could come up with some great ideas with all the neat stuff that she had inside it. There was lots of stuff in her bag. It had string, paper, glue, drawing supplies, and lots more.

Zoë sat down beside Alyssa as she watched the other three wrestle around on the den floor. "You three had better be careful," she said. "You don't want to get hurt! How would you guys like to do something with me for a change?"

"Like what? What do you have in mind?"

"Oh! I don't know. Let's check out my goody bag."

Zoë and the four children started to pull many things out of the goody bag. They started to pull out some light bulbs, toilet paper rolls, and some old newspapers. The children gave Zoë a weird look.

"What are we support to do with these? It's all garbage here."

"Well, listen up. First, we all go into the kitchen and grab us a big bowl. Then we add flour and some water. We mix the ingredients together to make a paste. On the dining room table, we'll tear the newspapers into strips. Then we'll place the light bulbs onto the toilet rolls. Then we dip the strips of newspapers into the paste and place them on the light bulbs and the toilet rolls."

She then started to demonstrate what to do while the paper was still wet and malleable. "See! This is called paper Mache. We can start by making a face on it. We continue with it until we have a puppet. Tomorrow, I will bring some other things so we can add hair and make outfits for each puppet. Now is everybody ready to get started?"

The children just gave Zoë another weird look, but they always loved to make a mess. The five of them start digging in with the puppet-making. The children were so excited that they couldn't wait to see how their puppets would turn out. This kept them busy all morning long.

Around lunchtime, Zoë asked them all if they could help clean up everything and place their puppets somewhere they could dry without breaking. The children started to make a fuss about cleaning up. They all loved to make the mess but didn't like to clean up afterward.

Zoë slipped down to the kitchen and began to get lunch ready for them all. She decided on mushroom soup. She poured out five bowls and brought them to the table. As everyone ate, Zoë questioned them about what they wanted to do that afternoon.

As usual, Alyssa was going to her room to lie down on her bed. As she got comfortable, she began to drift into her daydream once again and picked up exactly where she had left off.

Jack went under the house and grabbed his stash of money hidden there. Then his two best friends headed back to their home and did the same thing. The three friends then went to Playland Express. They walked the store, idly glancing at the many different electric things that were all around.

Jack stopped in front of the video game consoles. There were many games that went with the system. This store was like no other in the world. They had everything a kid could ever want—electronics, game consoles, MP3 players, and of course, all the games that went with them.

There was also a hangout for the kids in the back of the store. There, they could test out the products that they wanted to purchase from the store. They could hang out with friends and have some fun, too. There was even a staff member there just in case anyone needed assistance with anything. The staff would give any of them help with any kind of problem, whether it was about their home life, school, or games. It didn't matter what the problem was. They were there just to help out.

The children could purchase drinks and many different kinds of yummy treats as long as they cleaned up any messes they made in the process. No fighting was permitted. There were a couple of sofas that they could sit on, too. The trio eventually met up with some of their classmates at the back of the store. They each purchased a bag of chips and a soda. They sat down next to their friends and listened to what everybody was chatting about.

Jack quietly walked over to one of the staff members and asked if they could help him find a jeweler to turn his ruby into a pair of earrings and a pendent for a necklace for Mother's Day.

Jack showing the staff member a note from Zoe the babysitters that the money of 400.00 dollars was money he had saved up. That it was okay for him to spend it on Jewel for his mom.

Jack very nerves shaking slightly pulling his jar of money out of his book-bag showing the staff member and the rudy that he got from the miners.

Jack and a staff member proceeded to a nearby jewel store down the block.

Jack asks the jeweler if he could turn the Rudy stone into a pair of earring and a necklet for his mom and maybe even something small for his big sis. All I have is 400.00 dollars thou.

Jack was talking very quiet, looking towards the ground.

Staring down at Jack and the staff member that was with him and stated "Well, let's me see what I could do with this young man. That will come to 380.00 dollars young man." The Jeweler said.

"Here you go." Jack replied.

"Thanks young man, you can come back and pick them up in one week." The Jeweler said.

"Okay! Thanks." Jack replied.

Walking out the door Jack wipes his hands on his pants because they were all sweaty he was so nerves and was glad it was now over. With twenty dollars still in his pocket back to play land express they went.

After he took care of that, he rejoined his friends.

"Do you guys want to hear a story that I wrote?" Jack blurted out.

"Okay!" they all agreed.

"It's called 'Alligator Hunger!'" And then Jack stretched out his arms to set the stage and started his story:

"Here we are at Silver Spring," I said. "The tickets are paid for, and it's time to head into the park. I don't know why we don't go on the glass-bottom boat ride. I mean, we've been everywhere else—the lighthouse ride, the bird shows, the giraffes. We've even stopped to eat."

"Okay, we will go on the glass-bottom boat ride. Come on, everybody," I continued.

After ten minutes, we all said, "Phew, we made it."

"And if we go down a bit, we can press this button to radio the headquarters," the captain said. "Here you see a prop from a famous spy movie and other statues from the same movie—and look, there's an alligator resting on a rock. Ah, look, here's the gentleman who loves to talk about owls. Maybe we can learn more. Take it away, Bob."

Bob talked about the owls and other birds, and we all found it very interesting. "Well, time to go back," I said.

"What was that noise?" I asked. "It sounded like breaking glass! Or was it a creaking sound like the boards are old or something? But they couldn't have creaked in the middle of the spring like this. Why are my feet wet? And where did all this water come from? Please don't tell me the boat is sinking."

"Well, at least we can swim back to shore. What is pulling me down? Oh, no, it's a gator."

"I need air," I said, panicking. "I must get air. If not, I will die in this swampy spring water. I could lure the gator onto the shore and get air, or I could go with the gator to the center of the earth. I'll have to risk it. But how will I get to the crack in the earth? I know! I will have to swim to the crack. Well, there goes the gator."

But then more gators came.

I held my breath until I thought that my lungs would burst into dust, and then I saw the light from above my head. Just then, I passed through a huge hole in the ground.

I could still feel the gator's scales passing by my body, and my nerves were on edge. I was ready to fight for my life.

Well, I came upon a strange shore and found the air was sweet to taste. The sky was a reddish pink, and the sand looked snowy white. I took my time to get myself dry and get my thoughts back together. I was wearing a watch with a compass, but when I went to use it, I found that it just kept going in circles.

I felt like the people on the boats and planes who had become lost in the Bermuda Triangle—completely lost and out of touch with life and with reality.

To be continued.

Jack finishes his chips and his soda. "I should be going now."

"Wait! When can you finish your story, Jack? We want to hear more."

"Hm! We'll have to see. I have to get going. My mom is waiting for me. See you later."

Alyssa, Jenny, and Carlos finally arrived at his home. They opened the front door and strolled inside. Once inside, they saw a table filled with all kinds of yummy stuff to sink their teeth into. Carlos's family welcomed the girls in and told them to help themselves to the appetizers that were laid out on the table. There were crackers, cheese chunks, and cold cuts, and of course, there were two different kinds of bread as well. To complete the table, there were different kinds of lip-smacking desserts, too. The family watched curiously as the girls helped themselves to some of the yummy food.

"This is excellent," the girls stated. "Thanks! We appreciate this very much."

Phil, Carlos's father, watched Jenny very closely. He was very curious to know where Jenny had come from. He had never seen anyone like her—that is, except once before. He was very curious if there were others out there in the world like the two who were in his living room.

"Jenny, why don't you tell us a little more about yourself?" Phil finally asked.

Jenny was getting pretty annoyed with people. They always requested the same old information about her. She wondered why they couldn't come up with new questions. Jenny sat down and crossed her legs. Then she took a couple of deep breath and told her story once more.

Phil walked over to Jenny, crouched down beside her, and gave her a bear hug. He then motioned to the girls to follow him down a narrow hallway at the far end of the house. He stopped and unlocked the door and went inside. He called the girls over and told them to turn on the light as they came into the tiny room.

At the moment, Jenny was not sure about anything. She was having a very hard time understanding her own feelings. She felt like butterflies were flying around in her stomach. In all her life, she had never felt like this before. She just couldn't understand what was happening to her; let alone why it was happening. No one had ever been affection with her before.

Nothing could prepare the girls for what they were about to see. Jenny's eyes grew bigger in size and started to fill up with tears as she glanced around the tiny little girl's room. There were a few pictures up on the wall of two babies that were almost identical. The only difference was that one was a boy and the other was a girl. The little girl's ears were bigger than the boy's though. Both babies had webbed hands and feet, too. Their noses were longer than most people's noses.

Jenny didn't completely understand what this man was trying to tell her or even what she was seeing. To her, it didn't make much sense. She just couldn't bring herself to understand what was going on around her.

Phil could see the confusion in Jenny's eyes. He disappeared for a moment, but he was back in a flash, a tiny box in hand. It looked like it would belong to a special little girl, but to whom exactly? Where was this special little girl now? Phil didn't say a single word. He just handed the tiny box over to Jenny and headed back to the living room.

The two girls glanced at each other for a moment. They were both wondering the same thing. Could this have been the family that Jenny had been searching for all this time? It had been a very long time since she had seen them. She didn't even remember them. Could it be true? Had they stumbled on her family by accident?

The girls turned around and started to follow Phil down the narrow hallway back into the living room, where the rest of the family was sitting and enjoying their lunch. The girls grabbed some more food from the table and rejoined the small family.

Phil started to tell another story that was similar to Jenny's. They had had a set of twin as the girls had seen in the pictures in the back room. She was indeed Carlos's twin sister. "We were able to take those few pictures of our little girl before the doctor's rushed into the room and took her away," Phil said. "After a couple of hours passed, they came back and told us that she had died due to complications. We sadly went home with our baby boy but not with our little girl."

Phil glanced over to his wife, Mary-Jane. Then he motioned for Jenny to open the tiny box she was holding. Inside the tiny box was one worn-out picture of the twins. Jenny studied the picture closely. Alyssa was amaze, because the photo suggested that Carlos and Jenny were newborn twins. Jenny tried really hard to fight back the tears that were forming in her eyes. Jenny finally understood what they had been trying to tell her. She was the little girl they desperately missed.

Mary-Jane then told Jenny that the family celebrated a birthday just for her every year, though they had thought that she had died at birth. Jenny, on the other hand, didn't even know when her birthday was or even how old she really was. Mary-Jane told her to turn the picture over.

Jenny did as she was told. On the back, there were two dates. The writing said that Carlos and Jenny-Anne had been born on April 9, 1990. Jenny had died on April 10, 1990.

Carlos expressed disbelief. He wasn't sure he understood exactly what happening. He just couldn't bring himself to believe the news. He ran out the front door and disappeared into the woods.

Jenny ran after him. She knew exactly where he was headed, for she had watched him quietly sitting in her favorite tree for months. She had always wanted to talk to him before but was an afraid of doing so.

Jenny quietly approached Carlos. She placed her hand on his shoulder and said, "You're not alone anymore. We can be there for one another. I know exactly what you're going though. Remember, we are twins. I, too, have been teased all my life just like you. Who knows—you and I might become best friends. Just give it a try."

Carlos lifted up his head and looked at Jenny, tears in his eyes. "Do you really mean that, or are you going to be like everybody else? Pretend to be my friend and afterward tease me or take off and never come back?"

The two of them sat there and chatted up a storm. Carlos began to discover that the closeness he had always felt in the forest was real. Jenny had always been there, watching him high above in a nearby tree. After some time had passed, the two reunited siblings headed back to the house, where everyone was waiting patiently for their return. They crept quietly back into the house with puzzled looks on their faces as they approached their parents.

"Why?" they asked at the same time.

"Sit down, you two, and let us explain what happened so long ago. We wanted to have a baby very much. We heard about these doctors who were trying to make a perfect human. We volunteered with the experiment in hopes of having a baby. As it turned out, we were having twins. We were thrilled when the doctors told us. We wanted nothing more but to have you both after you guys were born. The doctors noticed that there was something different about you both. After a couple of hours, they came in and took Jenny away. They said that they wanted to run some tests. Later that night, they told us that Jenny had died, because she had something call chimera."

"What on earth is chimera?" all the children inquire.

"Well, let me continue. Everybody in the world has one set of DNA, which you get from your parents, but someone with chimera has two sets of DNA. Carlos and Jenny have two sets of DNA. They have human and animal DNA. That is why you two look so different from everybody else in the world. You two are very special, and we would never change anything about you. Well, that is everything, I guess. Do you guys understand what I just told you?" Mary-Anne asked after she had finished her explanation.

All the children responded with a yes.

Alyssa then got ready to continue on her journey. As she was gathering up her things, Mary-Anne handed her a goody bag to take with her. Alyssa was very grateful that her friend, Jenny, had found the family she had been desperately searching for.

She said farewell to them all and began to skip down the path toward the forest.

Susan pulled into the driveway and got out of the van. She strolled into the house, sat down at the dining room table, and began to make a list of the things they would need to take with them to the cabin.

Jack rode up the road and threw his bike on the front yard. He race into the house with his new video game.

"Hello, Mom!" he said.

"Jack, go pack the things you want to take with you to the cabin. Mark and Paige are coming, too. Can you ask your sister to do the same? She's still in her room."

Jack went upstairs and did exactly what he had been asked. He knocked on his sister's bedroom door. As usual, there was no response. Jack tiptoed up to Alyssa and screamed in her ear, "Get up and pack."

Alyssa jumped out of her bed and started to chase Jack out of her room and down the hallway. She put him in a headlock when she finally caught up with him, and she rubbed his head until it hurt.

"That's enough!" Susan shouted from the bottom of the stairs.

The children went back to their rooms and began packing up their things for the trip to the cabin. This would be the first of many trips that they would take during the year. While the children packed, Susan started loading up the van.

Susan had pulled Alyssa asided to check to see if all the birthday party invitation to Jack party was handed out, which was being handling after Spring Break.

Mark, Paige, and Zoë all arrived around the same time and began to help loading up the van. Soon after that, Jack and Alyssa brought down their stuff and loaded it on top of the van.

Everyone finally piled into the van, and away they went. During their first stop, they grabbed something to eat and drink. They later stopped for gas and some snacks along the way. After they played some car games and watched some movies on a laptop, the children fell fast asleep.

After a couple of hours on the 401, Susan made a right turn. About an hour later, they arrived at their cabin off Kirkland Lake. Susan disappeared into the cabin right away. She turned on some lanterns to help everyone find their way around the cabin. Zoë woke up the children so that they could venture inside, too.

After everyone was settled into their sleeping bags, Susan put on a movie, and together, they watched television until all of them were asleep.

Chapter Six

RAINING FROGS AND FISH BAITING

The trio woke up bright and early to start another day. When they stepped out of the cabin, they glanced out over the lake. They could smell the spring dew that has condensed all around them as they breathed in the early morning air. The fog was so thick that they couldn't even see five feet in front of them.

The trio crept over to the van. Then they opened the side doors and pulled out their fishing rods, fishing nets, and pails. "Let's go searching for some frogs and dew worms," the three said in unison. Off the trio raced down the path toward the small creek in the area.

They chased all the frogs, bumping into each other, not really looking where they were running. They fell into the creek so many times that they ended up soaked to the bone. Nervous frogs were jumping all over the place. In fact, it looked like it was raining frogs. It definitely was a sight you had to witness to believe.

"Cool! We have to try this again. That was fun. I wonder if there are any more frogs around here," Jack said.

When Jack headed south, he came across a small Garter snake. He wrapped it around his wrist and headed back toward his friends. "Hey, guys, want to scare my mom?" Jack said as he held the snake high up in the air to show his friends. Paige had also found a small lizard and had brought it back to the cabin, too.

On the way back, they found a fishing bait store. "Hey! We don't need to find bait. Look over there," Mark said, pointing the opposite way.

When the trio returned to the cabin, they saw Susan and Zoë setting the picnic table for breakfast.

"How was the bait hunting? Did you find any juicy worms or some nice plump frog legs that we can cook up?" Susan questioned, Rubbing her hands together.

Paige and Mark glanced at each other, thinking the same thing. Jack thought he was going to frighten his mother with the snake. Of course, they were all chuckling to themselves.

"Sure thing. You have to come and check it out."

Susan approached Jack and said, "Give it your best shot."

Jack was always trying to come up with new ways of scaring his mother. He paused for a minute or two and then said, "Close your eyes, Mom, and hold out your hands."

Susan did as she was instructed by her son. Susan began to counts to ten like she had done so many times before. As she counted, Jack placed the Garter snake in her hands. The snake slithered slowly up Susan's arm. Susan immediately opened her eyes and said, "Aw isn't he cute?" She picked up the snake by its tail and watched curiosity as it twisted and turned.

Paige thought she would give it her best shot, too, and tried to scare Susan with her lizard.

"That's a cute little lizard you have there, Paige," Susan said. "You three had better go cleanup for breakfast before you do anything else."

Susan then walked into the cabin to wake up Alyssa. "Breakfast is ready. Come and get it."

Alyssa wrapped her sleeping bag around herself, stumbled out of the room, and joined everyone at the picnic table. She took a quick look around her surroundings. It was indeed a beautiful sight to see.

After they quickly cleaned up breakfast, the trio quietly tried to slip down to the lake.

"Not so fast, you three. You guys need to help unload the van first before you go off exploring once again," Susan said, catching them red-handed.

The trio made a little fuss. They really wanted to go fishing. That was obviously more fun than unloading the van. Everybody helped out with the unloading, though, and placed everything in its rightful place inside the cabin.

The trio then quickly snuck away from cabin without being detected. They went over to the van and pulled out the metal boat, oars, and all the fishing gear. They raced straight down to the waterfront of Kirkland Lake.

Susan watched from the window of the cabin as the three friends raced down to the lake, thinking that they had gotten away without finishing their chores. She lets out a small chuckle as she stood there and watched them load the boat into the water.

They tied up the boat and took up the oars as well as their fishing gear. Next, they put on their life jackets and hopped into the boat. Quickly, they untied the boat once and pushed it away from the dock.

Susan was about to unpack some of the things they had brought in from the van. Then she started to wonder where Alyssa had disappeared to. She started to search the cabin. Alyssa was nowhere in sight. Susan strolled outside to search around the property and see if Alyssa was out there somewhere.

Alyssa had grabbed her sleeping bag and had laid it out underneath a weeping willow tree. Susan soon saw her there and went back into the cabin to continue with tidying up.

As Alyssa stretched out in her sleeping bag, she closed her eyes. She could feel the warmth of the sun beaming on her face. Slowly, she slipped back into her adventure.

She skipped happily down the path. She then paused for a moment, because she could hear the sounds of a carnival nearby. She decided to check it out, but when she arrived at the carnival, it was closed. She took a walk around the nearby town, checking everything out that she could see. Then she headed back toward the carnival.

She soon found a shady spot underneath a tree near the front entrance of the carnival. While she relaxed, Jo-Anne snuck up to her.

"Hey, Alyssa, are you still on that journey you were having the first time we met?"

"Oh! Hi, there! Yeah, I'm still on it. I'm heading home. Thanks for asking. Are you going to the carnival, too, Jo-Anne?"

"Well, I was thinking about going. Want to hang out together, Alyssa?"

"Sure! Sound great to me. Let's go. I can enlighten you all about my adventure."

The ladies walked through the gates and purchased their tickets. They stood there, wondering which direction they should proceed with first. They head toward the food court to grab a bite before they went on any rides or played any games. Alyssa painted a picture of everything she had accomplished on her journey and described how much fun she was having to Jo-Anne.

"Sound like you is having a blast of a time, Alyssa. Good for you. Life is too short to sit around and do nothing."

The ladies then cleaned up their messes. They headed over to the ticket booth next. They purchased a couple of tickets and headed for the roller coasters. They went on the twilight ride, which was full of twists and twirls, ups and downs, and everything that went around.

"I don't think we should have eaten before we went on that ride. I feel like I'm going to hurl," Jo-Anne said afterward.

"Aw, come on, Jo-Anne. One more time! Please! Afterward, we can play some games if you care to."

"Okay! Once more, and that's it."

"Agree!"

The ladies went back on the twilight ride. Jo-Anne held her stomach both during and after the ride. Alyssa began to giggle and then said, "I've never known anyone who felt sick after a roller coaster ride before."

The trio cast their lines out into Kirkland Lake, hoping to get a few nibbles. After some time passed, Mark's line started to bounce, which was very strange. What on earth could Mark have snared? His line was going crazy. It was all over the place. Mark stood up and started to reel the catch in. Paige and Jack started to rock the boat. Mark tried so hard to keep his balance as he reeled in the fish, but it turned out to be so heavy that it pulled Mark right into the lake with a splash!

"Help me!" Mark squealed as he splashed about.

"Mark … just stand up," the other two shouted, trying so hard not to laugh at their friend.

Mark then stood up, and the water only came up to his knees. Mark felt so embarrassed that he began to blush. "This just had to happen in front of a girl," he swore under his breath.

Though Jack gave Mark the impression that he was going to help him get back into the boat, Jack and Paige instead turned the boat around and started paddling away from their friend. They simply started to play a game of tag, keeping the boat away from Mark.

Mark chased his friends around the lake, trying to get back into the boat and not scare all the fish away. But Jack and Paige had always loved to tease Mark every chance they got.

"Come and get it," Zoë hollered.

Alyssa opened her eyes for a split second but then quickly returned to her daydream. Mark started kicking the water high as he ran through the water to get back to the shore and the other two paddled back to the dock as quietly as possible.

Susan searched for a couple of towels to put around the trio, for they were now shivering. They soon joined Zoë and Susan at the picnic table. They loaded up the burgers and hot dogs with everything that was in sight. They guzzled down some chocolate milkshakes. They were already prepared to dash back down to the dock. They all turned to Susan to find out if it was okay to go back to the water.

Fortunately, Susan nodded her head okay. The three of them disappeared in a flash long before Susan could change her mind.

"Payback is coming your way, you two," Mark yelled as they all climbed back into the metal boat, untied it, and pushed off the dock. They baited their hooks once again and cast their lines out as far as they could.

Paige decided to turn on some tunes on her tiny radio, which she had brought on the boat. She turned the volume down low, though. The guys opened up the cooler, which had been filled with sodas of all types. They each grabbed a soda and waited quietly for a good part of the afternoon to see who would be the one to make the first catch of the day.

Alyssa and Jo-Anne headed toward the games. They then took turns playing the ring toss. After that, they went over to the basketball area and tossed a few balls though the barrels. Then they ventured over to the game where you threw balls over goldfish. Last but not least, they threw some darts at all kinds of balloons to see who could pop the most. When they got thirsty again, they walked over to the food court to grab another drink.

All of a sudden, Alyssa froze! She just couldn't believe her eyes. Right there in front of her was the place Jenny had called home for many years. She strolled over to the tiny cage. It was totally disgusting. Alyssa could feel the hurt and the pity in her stomach. Tears started to form in her eyes as she stood there, trying to imagine what it must have been like living in that cage.

Jo-Anne walked over to Alyssa, placed her arm around Alyssa to comfort her, and asked, "What is it? Are you okay, Alyssa?"

Alyssa just stood there as quiet as a mouse for a long time. "I need to grab another drink," she eventually said. "I'll tell you a very sad story about my adventure, but don't worry. It does have a happy ending. This might take a while, because this one part is very sad."

Alyssa traveled back to the food court and grabbed another drink, which she sipped on very slowly. Then she told Jo-Anne about her friend Jenny, how that cage over there had been where Jenny had called home until she had ran away, how Jenny was now with her family and very happy, too. She also told Jo-Anne that she was happy that she had been able to help her new friend.

It was starting to get dark, so the ladies said farewell to each other and then parted ways.

Mark's rod started to bend. "Here we go again!" Mark said and started to reel in his line. "It feels like it's a big one!"

"It must be catchy. I have a big one, too!" Jack roared with excitement.

"Well! Hang on to your hats, boys, because I caught a big one, too."

As the three friends reeled in their lines with a mighty fight, all of their lines snap into pieces, and Mark went flying headfirst into the lake once again. Jack and Paige fell over backward to the other side of the boat. They were both laughing hysterically now. They laughed so loud and rolled around so much that they, too, fell into the lake.

The three friends eventually climbed back into the boat. They fixed their fishing lines and baited their hooks once again and continued fishing.

Paige recommended that they find another spot, because they had probably scared all the fish away. The three friends start to head west in search of the best fishing spot they could find. "This looks like a great spot!" the boys agreed, Paige just rolling her eyes.

They cast their lines out again in the hopes of catching some supper. The stop they had chosen ended up being the perfect spot after all, because the trio managed to catch supper for everyone. Afterward, they pulled into the dock and tied up the boat.

They each grabbed the cooler, which was now weighed down with bass and mud pout. They all carried it up the dock, through a small pathway, and over a tiny hill. "That was hard work. Whew!" they said, and all collapsed to the ground when they finally reached the cabin, lying there as still as could while trying to catch their breath.

Susan then walked over to them, pick up the cooler, and headed over to the picnic table. She soon went off to search for some newspapers so that she could spread out the fish and clean them. When she found some, she placed the newspapers down on the picnic table. One by one, she began to cut off the heads and tails of the fish. After she gutted them, she put them into a bowl with flour and water. The fish were now ready to fry and then eat.

"Kids, go clean-up for supper," Susan said as she walked over to where Alyssa was fast asleep. She then gave Alyssa a tiny shake to snap her out of her daydream. "Supper is ready. Go clean up."

Everybody sat around the picnic table and enjoyed the freshly caught fish along with potato-and-macaroni salad Susan had already made. To wash it all down, they all had some ice-cold orange juice as well.

Afterward, they cleaned up the dishes, and Zoë said, "How would you guys like to work on our puppets? I brought some material so we can make outfits for them."

Sounds cool, the trio thought. They quickly retrieved the materials that they needed, laid them out on the table, and quietly began to work on their puppets again.

However, Jack managed to slip away without being caught. He went behind the cabin and grabbed some frogs that he had hidden in a small box. He tiptoed quietly into the cabin and searched for Alyssa's sleeping bag. He then slipped the frogs into his sister's sleeping bag, snickering the whole time. Quietly, he move back to the picnic table and began to work on his puppet. He managed to do all this without being detected, too. Everyone had been too busy tracing the patterns, cutting them out, and pasting them on their puppets. Zoë also had several different colors of yarn to make all kinds of hairstyles for the puppets.

When it started to get dark outside, Susan started a fire in the fire pit. Then she went back into the cabin to grab some popcorn. With the popcorn in hand, she began to pop the kernels over the fire pit. The children cleaned up their mess, and they each joined Susan by the campfire.

They passed the popcorn around as they all took turns telling jokes. Jack always loved to make up spooky ghost stories whenever he sat around campfires. Afterward, they all stretched out on the ground and stared into the midnight sky. They started to play some games at that point, seeing who could find the Big Dipper or the North Star, which was the brightest star up in the sky. They all searched for all the different patterns these tiny fireballs in outer space mapped out so brightly in the midnight sky.

It started to get pretty late, and considering everything that they had to finish in the morning, they decided that it was a good idea to head to bed.

Everyone climbed into their sleeping bags to settle down for the night. Jack started to count to himself, wondering on how long it would be before Alyssa started to scream.

Alyssa came out of the bathroom after she had brushed her teeth and then climbed into her sleeping bag. Jack waited patiently, rubbing his hands together. Then, all a sudden, all you could hear from miles was Alyssa hollering so loudly that she could have woken up the dead. "This means war, Jack!" After she jumped out of her sleeping bag, she started to chase Jack all around the cabin.

"You two need to pipe down. Not another word," Susan said as she continued to read her book.

Chapter Seven

ICE-COLD WATER AND A HOT SPRING DAY

Zoë couldn't sleep. She tried and tried again, but nothing seemed to work. *I might as well get a head start on the packing up the van*, she thought. She walked into the bathroom first, packed up everything that need packing. Headed toward the kitchen and then began to bag up any food that would spoil, placing the bags back into the refrigerator to keep cold.

She quietly walked around the living room, packing up whatever she could carry out to the van without making too much noise. She then rolled up her sleeping bag, because she wasn't going to use it anyway.

By now, it was early morning. She took a walk down to the dock and watched the sun coming up, starting yet another day. She then untied the small boat and dragged it up to the cabin. She placed it on some blocks and tied it down to make sure that it didn't blow away. She then threw a tarp over the small boat to protect it from the elements.

Everybody soon started to wake up. They rolled up their sleeping bags as they smelled the aroma of bacon and sausages sizzling over the open campfire. Still sleepy, everyone dragged themselves out of bed and sat down at the picnic table. Zoë had already started breakfast—eggs and toasts. Everyone enjoyed their breakfast and started planning what they were going to do before they headed home.

Each of them listened to the sounds of nature that they would sadly miss when they all headed back home.

After they cleaned up and finished loading up of the van, Susan decided that she would give the children one more adventure before they headed back to their small town.

She handed each of the children a piece of paper that had clues and instructions on it to find some treasure, which she had hidden during the night. The trio started running toward the creek where they had caught the frogs, running through the small creek. They briefly stopped at the fishing shop to check out the bait that they had.

Jack purchased a bag full of crickets to scare Alyssa with in the morning while she was daydreaming. He carried the bag of crickets in his left hand and immediately went back to playing the game.

The three kids quickly resumed their treasure hunt. Alyssa searched around the cabin and found an acorn, some string, and a box full of shredded paper.

Mark, Paige, and Jack found fish string by the dock and an old tarp, and they raced back up to the cabin to show Susan.

Susan retrieved the materials and asked everyone to pile into the van so that they could get started on their long trip home. Along the way, they sang songs and played "Eye Spy with My Little Eye" along the way. They even watched two movies to pass the time.

Alyssa, of course, slipped into her fantasy world once again.

As she skipped along the path, she caught a glimpse of her bike. *I must be near Matthew's place*, she thought. She stopped and tried to hear Matthew playing with his sisters again.

She picked up her bike and pushed it alongside her. Eventually, she decided to take a break and parked her bike while she sat underneath a maple tree to rest a bit and get out of the hot sun. She slowly sipped on some juice as she glanced around her. She closed her eyes and listened to the sound of nature playing its songs. Alyssa was completely relaxed then. She could feel little raindrops drip all over her face. The ice-cold water felt nice during the hot spring day.

Then she remembered that it wasn't raining at all. Where were all these drips of water coming fromAlyssa opened her eyes, and then came asplash.Alyssa was soaked as two water balloons tumbled down on her. There, up in the tree, were Matthew's little sisters giggling.

"Where did you two come from?" Alyssa asked.

The girls just giggled some more.

Alyssa then helped the girls down from the tree, and they disappeared in a flash.

"Now where did you guys take off to?" Then Alyssa remembered that the children in this family loved to play hide-and-seek. Alyssa moved stealthy around the tiny park. She looked behind every tree that she could find, and she left no stone unturned. As she stood there scratching her head, she wondered where the two little girls had disappeared to.

"Eek," Alyssa yelled, jumping two feet in the air. She turned around quickly, and there was Matthew, trying to give her a hug around her legs. She smiled sweetly at Matthew and returned the hug.

"How is everything going, Matthew?"

"Come see! We have a new home."

Matthew grabbed Alyssa's hand and dragged her to his new house. To Alyssa's great surprise, they were living in the village where the dwarfs were.

"Hey, you guys, it's time to stretch out your legs," Susan hollered behind her. She had just pulled into a small gas station off the freeway.

Everyone piled out of the van to stretch their legs. They all went into the tiny store to get some refreshments and have a bathroom break before they got back on the road.

Wherever they were, they could witness the beautiful colors that decorated the sky above. The air had a little chill. Everyone piled back into the van with their chips and pops. Soon, everyone was comfortable once again. They were all happy to be on their way back home, too.

The children sang some songs until they reached home. Once there, they helped unload the van. Jack asked if he could go down to Playland Express to hang out for a while, but what he really wanted to do was pick up his mother's necklace and earrings, which he had had made for Mother's Day. He also wanted to pick up an MP3 player for his big sis.

Paige and Mark dropped off their things at home and soon joined Jack at Playland Express. The three friends each grabbed a drink and a bag of chips and sat down with their classmates. Everyone was talking up a storm about what they had all done for their spring breaks. After all, tomorrow, it was back to school.

Alyssa tiptoed up to her bedroom and turned on the radio and lay down on her bed once again. While she was listening to the soft music playing on the stereo, she drifted back into her fantasy world once again.

Alyssa took Matthew's hand and walked over to the huge hut that was between the four tiny huts. Matthew opened the door. "Mom, look who's here to visit us again," he yelled.

Matthew's mom came running out of the kitchen with dough spread all over her hands. She had been in the middle of making chocolate chips and peanut butter cookies.

"Oh! Hi, Alyssa, it's always a pleasure to see an old friend. Come on in and make yourself at home. I'll be with you in a minute," she said and then disappeared back into the kitchen.

As Alyssa and Matthew sat down on the lounge, the door flew open, and the seven dwarfs and Matthew's two little sisters came running in toward them. They all sat down on the floor and listened to Alyssa tell them all about her adventure. Matthew's mom came in with some refreshments for everyone and some homemade peanut butter cookies for all of them to munch on. They continued to listen to Alyssa talking about her adventure.

The trio later drove their bikes to Harvey Park. After they parked their bikes, they raced over to the monkey bars and hung upside down on them.

They talked about the invention that they had been working on together all week. They agreed that they would continue working on the project for however long it took to finish. They would work on the invention after school and throughout the summer until they had it working.

The three of them then hopped on their bikes and had a bike race over the hills and though the mud puddles. They rode around the neighbourhood, checking things out. They stopped at the pile of gold that they had hidden underneath the tree. They pick up the gold and rode back to Jack's place and hid the pile underneath his house. Next, they ran into the house to get cleaned up.

You could smell the aroma of sweet chilli cooking throughout the house. "Mm! Smells delicious in here," they all said at once.

"Kids, it's almost suppertime," Susan hollered.

As everyone sat around the table and ate, Susan reminded Jack and Alyssa to have a bath before they went to bed. "Aw, Mom, do we have to?" they both protested together.

Zoë then requested that after supper, they all finish up their puppets. Everyone helped clean up after supper. Then they retrieved their puppets and went back to the dining room table to begin working on them.

In the meantime, Susan did some work on the computer in the den.

Zoë started to build a tiny stage so that the children could put on a puppet show for Susan when they were finally finished making the final touches on their puppets.

The children were laughing and carrying on. They each decided to make their puppets very weird and funny-looking. When everybody was done, they cleaned up their mess and went into the living room to help Zoë with the stage. Susan joined the children in the living room so that she could watch their puppet show.

Ladies and Gentlemen boys and girls have a seat owner show is about to start.

The day at the park

Zoe: Kids how would you like to go feed the ducks today?

Paige: Sure, I'll bring some kites with me. We can fly them afterwards.

Mark: I'll bring the blanket.

Jack: I got the bread crumb.

Alyssa: I've got the food.

Zoe: Well, it looks like we're ready to proceed to go the park to the duck and off they skipped happily down the pathway.

The End

Afterward, Susan told them that they had done a wonderful job on the puppet show. "You all should be very proud of yourself for a job well done."

Susan slipped into the kitchen to make some snacks for everyone to munch on before Mark and Paige headed for home. Everyone laughed up a storm while they munched on some cheese and crackers and sipped on some hot chocolate. Afterward, Mark and Paige grabbed their puppets, and out the door they went as they said farewell.

Jack and Alyssa took their puppets to their bedroom, and then they went off to their separate bathrooms to have their bath before they headed off to bed.

Susan helped Zoë clean up the mess in the living room. She paid Zoë for all the help she had given over the past week and then said good night to her as she closed the door behind her slowly.

Susan then went into the den and packed up her notes for work and stuffed them into her briefcase. She then headed upstairs and checked on the children.

She finally soaked in a hot bubble bath before she went to bed herself. She climbed into bed with a great book, began to read for a while, and soon fell fast asleep.

Chapter Eight

DREAMS CAN BECOME REALITY

Jack and Alyssa woke up to start their first day back at school after their spring break. Ecstatic, Jack just couldn't wait to go. All of sudden, he felt something crawling all around his legs. He slowly lifted up his blankets to see what was crawling on his legs and then he let out a scream, quickly jumping out of his bed. His bag of crickets had been opened, and they had gotten loose in his bed.

Alyssa, on the other hand, just lay there on her bed, feeling a little bit depressed about going back to school. After all, what was she going to tell everybody she had done for spring break? Really, she had just lain around doing nothing.

Jack came running into her room. "Get up, you lazy bones!" he shouted, and then he flew downstairs to join his mother in the kitchen and grab some breakfast.

Alyssa slowly moved around her room like a snail. She finally found something to wear. She crept quietly down the stairs and mumbled good morning to her mother and brother.

Everybody cleaned up their dishes afterward, grabbed their schoolbags, and raced out the door.

The school bus was just turning the corner as they all walked out the front door. The children climbed abroad the bus, and Susan drove off in the van to work.

Jack, Paige, and Mark checked out what they would have for lunch. They started to trade things from their lunches with each other like they had done since the beginning of school.

Alyssa turned on her MP3 player and stared out the window until they reached their school.

Everyone piled out of the bus and raced to their favorite spots in the school yard to hang out until the morning bell made its loud ringing.

Alyssa stood there, frozen for a minute as she took a quick look around the school yard. She just couldn't understand what she was looking at. She gave her head a tiny shake to wake up, but she wasn't dreaming. Standing there, she tried to understand what she was seeing.

Little Curtis snuck up behind her and grabbed her legs to give her a big hug hello. Alyssa jumped about two feet in the air and let out a screech that was so loud everybody turned their heads toward her. Alyssa began to blushing.

Then the school bell rang, and everyone lined up to go inside. As everyone headed to their classrooms, Alyssa took Curtis to his kindergarten class. After all, she was his reading buddy. She then headed toward her own classroom.

Miss Kirkwood stood there, staring at her students, and decided to assign them a thousand-word essay about what they had done for spring break.

Alyssa let out a small chuckle. *Yeah, right!* She thought as she stared at the blank piece of paper on her desk. *What on earth can I write about? All I did was lay around and do nothing. Some essay this is going to be.*

As the recess bell went off in the hallway, you could hear the younger grades running up and down the hallway to get out into the school yard.

Alyssa wished she, too, could go out outside, for she wasn't getting anywhere with her essay. She glanced keenly out the window as she watched all the young children laughing and running around the school yard.

Jack and his two best friends headed toward the northwest end of the school yard by the fence. Mark noticed a door somewhat covered and buried in the ground. He let out a small chuckle and pointed toward the door. "Hey, guys, take a look at this! Where do you think it leads to?" Mark looked at his friends with question marks in his eyes, wondering where the door went.

"Don't know," the other two responded.

And then the bell rang again!

All the children in the school yard started to line up so they could proceed back to their classrooms.

"We should check it out at lunchtime and see where it leads to," Jack suggested. Paige and Mark agreed with the plan.

Miss Kirkland walked up behind Alyssa and observed what she had done so far on her essay. "What's wrong? You haven't written a single word for your essay, Alyssa," Miss Kirkland commented as she knelt down beside Alyssa.

"I really don't know what to write about."

"Take your time. It will come to you," Miss Kirkland said as she placed her hand on Alyssa's shoulder and then walked away.

In no time at all, it was lunchtime. Everybody packed up their books and grabbed their lunches.

Alyssa slowly walked outside and glanced around the school yard. She noticed one of her good friends was running the track like she had always done in the past. Just then Alyssa realized that it was her friend, Alice, who was really Jo-Anne in her daydream. Alice had always talked about going to the Olympics someday, for it was her dream to represent Canada.

Alyssa momentarily looked around again. She saw a set of twins standing in a corner of the school building, and a bunch of older kids were teasing them. These twins had a health problem called Down syndrome. They didn't look, talk, or act like anyone else at school.

Alyssa walked over to the group of kids and told them that it wasn't nice to tease other people just because they were different. She explained that everyone was special in their own way.

Alyssa hung out with the twins for a little while and realized that Jenny and Carlos in her dreams had really been these twins from school.

Jack, Paige, and Mark took their bag lunches and again headed to the northwest end of the school yard near the fence.

Mark put his lunch down and started to fiddle with the lock on the door that opened into the ground. After some time passed, the lock finally broke open.

The trio looked at each other and then glanced around them to see if the coast was clear. Once they were certain that no one was watching them, they opened the door and snuck inside.

Their eyes grew bigger, for they couldn't believe what they were seeing. There were costumes everywhere. They each grabbed a costume and put it on. Jack instantly became a knight. Mark became a king of France, and Paige put on the queen's outfit.

They sat there, eating their lunches as they all wondered why they had never had school plays in the auditorium. Where had all these costume come from anyway?

Jack told his two friends that his mother had once told him that their school had had a fire a long time ago. The school had lost over half of its building, and they had rebuilt a new section of the school as a result.

Surprised, Paige said that she had heard the same story from her own parents. Maybe this was the basement of the old school, and everybody had forgotten about it.

The three of them packed up their lunches and came back out to the school yard. They decided to speak with the principal about what they had found. Maybe they could ask if the school could put on a concert at the end of the school year.

After they pitched their idea to the principal, it was time to head back to class.

Alyssa surprised Miss Kirkland, because her hand was now moving a hundred miles a minute. She now knew what she was going to write about. Naturally, she decided to write about her daydream.

By the end of the day came to an end, everybody dragged their heels. All the children piled back onto the buses.

Alyssa and Jack both eventually got off the bus, but when they turned around; they saw that most of their friends were getting off the bus, too.

Then it hit Alyssa that their friends were getting off here for Jack's birthday. She had forgotten all about it. So had Jack, she guessed.

As the children approached Alyssa and Jack's house, the door opened. There, waiting to greet them all was a clown. He showed all the children where they could put all their book bags, and then he asked them to follow him into the backyard.

The backyard was full of different tables of fun actives to finish. There was even a water balloon table full of balloons to throw at Mr. Brown, too. There was an arts and crafts table run by some of the mothers. There was also a ring toss and lots more.

Susan was busy in the kitchen, getting things ready for the big birthday surprise. She went into the living room and started to fill the table with boxes of fried chicken, juice boxes, fries, and salad.

When Susan had everything ready, she called, "Come and get it." Everyone raced into the house, grabbing paper plates and filling them up with all kinds of yummy stuff to eat.

Next, it was time for the birthday cake, ten candles lighting it up. Everyone sang "Happy Birthday" to Jack. Afterward, Jack opened his presents.

Everybody helped clean up the house and yard after the birthday party. Then the grown-ups and their children headed home.

Jack and Alyssa carried all the birthday presents up to Jack's room. Then they got ready for bed. Susan called them downstairs so that they could all curl up together and watch one of Jack's new movies with a big bowl of popcorn.

Afterward, they all headed for bed. As they lay awake in their beds, the children began to wonder what the summer holidays would bring. *If spring break could be this much fun*, they wondered, *what kind of adventure would they have in the summertime?*